COME COME

Come come

by
Jo Jones

 Sheba Feminist Publishers

First published by Sheba Feminist Publishers,
488 Kingsland Rd, London E8 in October 1983

British Library Cataloguing in Publication Data
Jones, Jo
Come, come.
I. Title
823'.914[F]   PR6060.0/

ISBN 0-907179-17-7

Typeset in Plantin 11/12 by Range Left Photosetters (TU)
01-251 3959

Printed and bound by A. Wheaton and Co Ltd, Exeter

To Violette Leduc

1. Shut Up

The gods are just, they say, or tricksters, they say:
they trot towards spilt blood and wine and wailing.
They grant your three wishes: yes, they feed you:
but whose are the small bones on the plate when
your belly is full? Your girl of gold chinks in others'
pockets, and who hears when you sing in your
Cassandra trap?

My tongue is forked in my mouth, it stings twice,
once with its own antidote, wide of the striking
centre. Give me a language to speak, that is, save
me, save me: and I will give you my soul after death,
my first born, ten years of my life, my eyes.

As in the best stories.

She learned to ride a bike on a path by the edge of a precipice.

Her grandmother unpicked the stitches of the sleeves in her two viyella dresses; it was so hot, that summer, in the north of Norway. Her little plump arms speckled egg-brown.

She was seven; her aunt's bicycle was much too big and heavy for her to learn on, but she had no idea that anything in this world could be too big or heavy for her. She never has learned. It's about time.

Yes, take it Aagot, her aunt said. Go up on the top path, it's not so stony. Bring it back safe, I need it to go to the village in the morning. Be careful.

Be careful? Aagot knew about stones and about falling over, her knees were scraped from climbing. The stones didn't hold steady, that was the trouble. The world moved about under her feet. It didn't stop her from climbing when what she wanted, a short cut, a clump of blue flowers, was at the top.

She was small. Her head was as high as the saddle. She reached up to the handlebars, pulled and wheeled. It surprised her that the bicycle moved wilfully, trying to take its own choice of direction, not hers. The path from the house sloped down, because she was not going to the top path as her aunt had told her. The bicycle wheeled her, ran her, down to the gate, the pedal tangled with her leg, and brought her down. It hurt, but nothing much to show, only some grit scratches on the palms of her hands and some bruises for the next day.

The problem was how to pick the bike up. She tried lots of ways, but each time it bucked and slipped. She circled it with pleasure; that doesn't work, what next? She was pink and brown and slippery with heat, and mucky too, and I love her and wish I had seen her, little girl, little girl.

The rake was on the ground in the bean patch. A few cabbage seedlings snapped under her blunt little feet. She pushed the rake handle under the back strut of the bike, pulled the rake up with both hands, leaned the rake head against her shoulder while she reached back for the gate, jerked the gate towards her knowing that it dragged in a rut in the path, rested the rake head against the gate, walked round the bike and grunted it upright.

Who taught her these three things: that sullen heavyweights can be tricked; that a rake can do more than the limits of its name; that you don't ask for help if you can do without it? The locking of things, the traps of words, the tackle of dignity. They had taught her, at seven, the opposite: she was perverse. She perseveres. She knew these things, good gifts wished on her in her cradle; no spiteful black figure then, the forgotten guest, to open the door and spoil with a But. Sticks and stones don't break her bones and nothing I say hurts her. One new thing she had just learned; you wheel a bike with the top weight angled towards you. If you are only seven and small it is easier to right if it moves onto you than away from you. You don't let heavy things carry you with them when they crash onto the stones.

So she takes the weight, shoulders and manipulates. Aagot will use this skill again to save herself, her life, when she moves across other stony places and is beckoned to be broken. She uses it too as Hecka's lover, bending and controlling, leaving her free. Again she is slippery and brown, golden pink, sprinkled with toast crumbs from eating in bed. She has a small blue scar for life on her knee, from the day she learned to ride a bike on the narrow path by the precipice with rocks and sea below at her side. Her scars are for life. Many of Hecka's are against it.

Why did she take that monster bike to such a ledge when there was a safe path above the house?

It was nearer to the house, she says. She doesn't see any reason in going out of her way to avoid danger.

How did she save herself, when her small hands can't have stretched to pull on the brakes?

She can't remember.

She must have learned many tricks that day, to save herself and to get what she wanted. When she was thirsty and mistress of the bicycle, she went back to the house. Her aunt saw her coming the wrong way. A trap was set for her. Had she seen anyone while she was out playing? Aagot guzzled a mug of water. No. She didn't know that her cousin Per had come to the house and that they must have seen each other if she had been on the top path. She was scolded. It didn't hurt much.

The trouble was she hadn't practised to deceive. And it does need a lot of practice, which she got in later years, in her affaires and marriage most particularly. Then she began to learn about traps, how to save herself from them and get what she wanted. She was scolded, briefly disliked because no one likes a lying little girl, given bread with thick marmite to eat in bed and slept intact, crumbed, getting up once in the night to drink more water, sleeping again with dreams which left no memory because she did not need them to make a story of her days.

Of course in later years she tried to give up the unsuitable habit of pedalling in wide arcs and scraping to a halt on her own heels. She got married and learned to sit in, and on lucky days navigate from, the passenger seat of her husband's car. This was OK since he was thrusting gears, turning the wheel, stopping and starting, deciding to make a journey and deciding its destination. If she asked for the car to be stopped so she could go to a lavatory or a shop, he obliged: pulling up sharp with the butt end of the car sticking out, and keeping the engine running. When she came back the car would leap forward before she had shut the door. Seat belts were not allowed; to wear one questioned his ability to drive and his right to control. Even the possibility of death lay in his hands.

It was far from sure if Aagot existed at all. She was surprised when the mirror showed her the same image day by day. She tried so hard to smile and comply, to bend with every force which pulled her.

'Can we stop and get some aquavit? The Edvardsons drink it and we're low.'

Double fault. She should have remembered before. He had to stop the car. Engine running, a queue in the shop, bumper stuck out in the traffic; a crash of denting metal, doors slammed, shouted accusations, Aagot standing on the pavement clutching a bottle and knowing she was somehow the cause of so much trouble and the rage was against her. She was frightened. It was the beginning only, the reason why being acted out, the passion topping to take effect after the public ritual was over. She stood with a silly placatory

5

smile clutching the bottle. Other people standing watching may have experienced a useful little catharsis.

Names and numbers were exchanged. She slipped into the passenger seat and braced her legs for the neck-break start. There was silence and a lot of unnecessary manoeuvring on the way home. While he was opening the front door she dropped the bottle and it smashed.

Most menacing of all, he stood to one side so that she entered first.

Aagot doesn't remember who spoke first, what words came, some did, any would have done. She remembers him saying 'You're lucky you're not married to a violent man'; She remembers wondering why. Then a blow which knocked her over, broke two of her front teeth and bled her nose. He went to the kitchen, perhaps fulfilled, or ashamed, or to stop himself performing the full extent of his disgust.

If a man faces up to violence it's courage: if a woman does it's masochism. Aagot got up, called after him in a steady voice 'You've broken my teeth', picked up the nearest thing, a sock, to catch the blood from her nose and lip, and went after him into the kitchen. The door was not opened for her. She didn't want to be hurt any more, but she realised what she had always known and long forgotten.

An absurd scene: she pacing behind him arguing calmly and he in a rage aiming blows which she parried with her arms, still talking. The pine egg-frame was knocked from the wall: he: look what you've done, always smashing things; her feet crunching over the slime and shell, mayhem happy amongst the minor breakages. When the bleeding from her face stopped she put a kettle on to make herself, and herself alone, some coffee. He left the kitchen.

I love her and am proud of her. What she did was finely judged. It would not be so for all women at all times, but then it was. Yes, I do realise it is an offence against modern love, that meaningful relationship, to be proud for another: I do not own her: claims and demands are outrageous: indifference is the in-difference, and I am growing old, which is stupid, in a world which is young and therefore wise.

I nodded acquiescence until I fell off the wall, I'm falling, still falling, plummet, and it's better down here than it ever was, this no-man's land. I'll crack the system if it doesn't break me first. There's glory for you.

Aagot saved herself and got what she wanted. He cancelled the dinner party for that evening. Apart from the fact that they still hadn't got the drink for the Edvardsons, he couldn't have his dignity spoilt by her appearance, and she couldn't be trusted to collude in a story about an accident with the car, which was how he saw it. She kept grinning at his story, which opened her lip again and let fearful streams of blood run down her face and throat.

In fact, she couldn't be relied on any more.

She is small and dresses in fawns and blues and greys like the colours of most constant things. Hecka needed the flamboyance of black, red, purple, bright yellow, unstable things, to be sure; Aagot mocked her and she hurt. She again and she, she predicates, never enough. Hecka liked her whisky neat, her tobacco unfiltered, her food polysaturated, Aagot unspared, crying; riding her in victory laughing, which she shared because Hecka gave it to her; frightened for what she would do next and willing her to do it.

She does not make stories of her experience or gain power from the kind of lies and puffs and extractions which Hecka needed. She never knew what she had done by acting as a competent simpleton, the kind who learns to ride a bike on a cliff edge; a stubborn idiot who moves into danger with no desire to be harmed.

Dark blue volvos are the perfect violence machine, as featureless there as fawn raincoats, blue eyes. This was all the description people had. A dark blue volvo, three men, two middle-aged one young, fair brown hair. The police were puzzled by the frozen simplicity, the lack of normal recall. No more description came from the women after rest and sedation.

The technique was simple. In the late afternoon a blue volvo would pull up in a quiet street, a man would wind down the window and call to a woman walking near 'Excuse me . . . we're trying to find . . .' and hold out a piece of paper. Any helpful woman would go over to try and direct them. While she spoke to the driver or the man in the front passenger seat the third man would open the rear door and pull her in. He, the strongest of the three, would deal with her screams or struggles with a sharp blow. His special interest was inflicting pain. He did not rape or apparently want to. The other two did this to the woman. She would be thrown onto a lonely roadside, bruised, bleeding, and needing many days before the fear of death receded. Three such women were interviewed by the police. The fourth woman was fourteen and had such internal injuries that her ability to bear children in future was doubtful, which caught the blunted public imagination. Men were disgusted and women terrified, and the police took it seriously. The drivers of dark blue volvos were stopped and asked to co-operate in accounting for their movements on certain nights. The enquiries failed. The three men celebrated their success by attacking another woman and throwing her out of the car outside a police station. She was bruised and torn and her wrist broken and she got very little sympathy because many warnings had been given not to walk alone after dark. Strange for a curfew to be imposed on the possible victims and not the possible attackers, but no one questioned it.

Like most other people, Aagot read of these events and talked of them at work and with women friends, but not with her husband. He believed that there were decent men, the majority, of which he was one, and a very small number of bad ones, exaggerated by a press which was cynical in its search for upsetting news and by women who were hysterical in their illogical fears, in the making of connections between these and other acts of cruelty, connections which might even include him.

She told Hecka as of no special account. She tells unscaled narratives. What she told then was like a rider, a trivial parallel put in for conversation's sake. She told Hecka who had come home sick and angry after an average ordinary assault; oh yes, I've been there too, it seemed she was saying. It took some minutes to hear that she was telling something so extraordinary that Hecka had to demand more and more of her to believe it was true. After where, when, what, the

8

impossible why. She said: 'I don't really know, I didn't think about it.' Think now please Aagot. 'I can't remember.'

I try to give her linear account but she would disagree with what I read into it, saying that it is histrionic, overblown, flaunting the purple and yellow.

A dark blue volvo drew up slowly ahead of her on the far side of the road, in the dim evening. She had been visiting friends and they had talked about the attacks, and she came away feeling upset that she alone was angry. The others were ill at ease about it; it was indelicate, they didn't know whose attitudes to express. One of the women knitted right through the talk and Aagot found that powerfully insulting. She learned to knit.

If you will not take possession of your own story then you give it to me. It is mine now. I love you and can grab from you what you are not offering, just as I can take from an enemy what I will. The outcries and acts of love and rage keep me alive and kicking.

A man leaned out from the driver's seat, waved a piece of paper at her, and beckoned for her to help.

She crossed over.

As she walked she knew what was happening, yes: no, it was not absentmindedness nor disbelief. She was frightened, that she can say. She was aware in those few steps of moving into a dark and bloody centre, and she chose. She was an accomplished actress. Once you know how, it's a skill you don't lose, like riding a bike. She was pushing her art to its limits. Was she so sure of herself? She's not sure.

She smiled, walked flirtatiously, offered herself, and looked very hard to remember. She reached for the door and let herself in before the man in the back seat could make his special move.

The Dreadful Has Already Happened, says the amiable psychologist. He knows about the pain of childhood but has not been much near death, specific pain, gross evil. If the Dreadful had already happened it can surely happen again and often does. You trample on all the lovely dead women with your comfort. The real world is the world we die in.

9

I stumble in a clumsy circle lunging and grabbing and grab what I can. We may die for a cause, fighters, fools forgotten, but at the last we must know that death makes nonsense of all theory, all the reasons why. Death is not an event in life. She chooses to risk being unborn, no one of that name, to walk from the broad safe plain to the narrow crumbling ledge where she knows herself more clearly with each step to the last shifting foothold where she grips smallest and brightest and she makes of this deadly game an event in her life.

Did she open the door, seduce, trick and win for the sake of other women? She can't remember. Honestly she can remember nothing. It was no use for Hecka to storm and demand. She looked at her pale slenderness. Aagot lowered her eyes. There was something she did not tell. I am glad, a secret, she showed it but did not give it away to peel raw and ruin.

She was raped by two of the men, if you can call it rape; afterwards the law went into tremors about definition because she had consented. The third man was disgruntled so she flattered him and watched carefully to see that he was happy. At the right time she held out promises of future pleasures. Her mouth was dry. She stroked, coddled, smarmed, and they loved it. She circled and manipulated, clever child, wise woman.

At the last she asked for a phone number so they could fuck again soon. She looks up quickly, fierce blue joy. They gave it.

Her husband was confused, then proud of her and said she was one hell of a woman, too loudly and too often, then left her. She came out of it without glory because she had not suffered enough.

She spills crumbs and coffee and tobacco shreds in her lover's house and bed, but keeps her house clean and empties the ash trays others soil there.

I think she needs me.

My purple florid babbling mess tells her story. She oversees and keeps me in mind of the detail which makes my story a lie.

I need her.

10

I would lay down my life for a good lie or lie all my life for a good lay; it's the same nice knock-down. My trouble until I die is that I must struggle to feel that I have the right to have been born and the worth to go on living. I will never win, my limits are as delicate as an egg shell still forming, the essence dribbled out known and ugly, by the slightest tap of misfortune. The only grace I have is to recognise the winged and free when I see it and to suffer that I am injured by the sight.

How does Aagot live now, knowing what she does? Sometimes she cries, for no present hurt and cannot say why. Her eyes dull, her head drops, her hands lie limp and open. Death nearly claims her again. It is a slow and dangerous way backing along the narrow path and she must walk it many times and always alone. I cannot guide her reverse steps: 'Come . . . come'. A word out of place, a slip of the tongue, a step out of true, could unfoot and break her. She backs slowly, testing each stone that there is solid ground beneath. I am not there to take her hand.

There can be no stories there.

*   *   *

2. Good Questions

Burst now, storm, she is about to come . . . Wild
gestures from the trees, the necessary wind before
the storm; oh let her come in now, let there be an
end to it.

Violette Leduc

'I fancy making some marmalade,' Hecka had said at the party, 'but I don't know how.'

'You? Why on earth . . . ?' a friend began to say. This was the question Hecka wanted: so she could tell how she was inclined to a bit of one-off housewifery with something bottled to show for it.

But Aagot took it as a request for information. She moved across the room to Hecka and Hecka prickled.

'You need seville oranges to make marmalade,' Aagot said.

'What are seville oranges?'

'The kind you need to make marmalade.'

Hecka grinned, and discovered that Aagot wasn't joking.

'It seems a long way to go. Perhaps I'll bake a cake.'

'No, you get them in a market. It's the proper time of year. I could get you some easily. You can use grapefruit and some lemon too. Have you got a preserving pan?'

Hecka was uncomfortable. She was hoist. She could see a friend across the room amused at her discomfort.

'Well, thanks,' said Hecka.

On Saturday there was a phone call. Aagot said who she was because they did not know each other well.

'Hello, it's Aagot. I found some seville oranges and I bought two pounds for you and two pounds for me. I've got them here. Shall I bring them over?'

Hecka had not any intention of making marmalade.

'That's very nice of you,' she said, 'but you mustn't go to the trouble of bringing them over. Give them to me when we see each other again.'

At least, she thought, I can eat them. She didn't know how bitter a fruit they were.

'But when will we meet again?' said Aagot.

It was becoming intricate.

'I don't know.'

'Then we should fix something.'

'Mm, yes. Well, I'd better come and get them sometime.'

'When?'

'When would suit you?'

'I'm in this evening.'

Hecka was discouraged by this willingness to do service.

'I'm afraid I can't this evening.'

'Tomorrow then?'

'Yes, OK, thanks. What time?'

'I'm out until 8.30 at a meeting. Could you come then?'

The obligation, it seemed to Hecka, was growing. She had to disturb a tired and busy woman who had to go to a meeting on a Sunday night. There was at least one other scheme working which she did not think of.

'Well, all right, thanks, if it's not too late for you.'

'Oh no, that's quite all right.'

Aagot gave her address.

'It might be difficult for me to get home. It needs two buses.'

Hecka was making an inept retreat from something which was closing in on her.

'I can give you a lift home.'

'Oh no, that's too much. I'll come, I won't stay long.'

'You should try orange and grapefruit, that's very nice,' said Aagot.

'Perhaps I will,' Hecka lied.

'Tomorrow then, 8.30.'

'OK. Thanks a lot.'

Hell, she thought, I'm just a girl who can't say no; and she began to wonder.

She arrived five minutes early because you can't be sure of timing a two bus journey. Aagot appeared upset by the early arrival.

On the kitchen table was a bag with some rather nasty looking oranges. And a grapefruit.

'That's nice,' said Hecka, feeling sillier by the moment, 'but you shouldn't have got the grapefruit. I could have done that.'

'And I've written out the recipe for you,' said Aagot.

Hell's Teeth.

'Would you like some coffee?'

'Thank you.'

In the circumstances she was obliged to accept anything, a request for a fiver, the story of Aagot's life. While the coffee was making Hecka looked at her. It was clear she had dressed

16

carefully, her trousers blue velvet, the top rather special, her hair clean and groomed, presumably for the meeting she had been to. Hecka listened politely to extra instructions on greasing the pan, testing for set, different methods for assuring that there was enough pectin. Courtesy wiped out honesty. Painstaking kindness wiped the floor with her. She nodded pretence of interest: she owed it.

On the table was a fresh quiche and a bowl of salad with nuts, red peppers, green stuff. Both were covered with transparent sealing film. Two plates also. Hecka was very hungry. She had forgotten to eat that day. She envied the guest expected.

'Are you hungry? Would you like something to eat?'

It would be impossible to shatter the quiche, trouble the salad. For a start impossible to be responsible for peeling off the seal of film.

'No, no, thanks, I'm OK.'

She drank her coffee, took her oranges, declined a lift home, and went.

Weeks later she discovered that Aagot had plotted every detail for her alone. The clothes were selected for her, real coffee made instead of instant, and the food was for her to eat. There was no other guest coming. Afterwards, disappointed, Aagot had made the quiche and salad last for three days and had eaten every mouthful with resentment and sadness, believing an express invitation had been refused.

* * *

Hecka was ill at the winter's end. She went to work for three weeks dragging herself through a performance of her days. No one seemed to notice how poorly the acting was.

She lost more weight, which paid no compliments to her ageing face but made her clothes hang, or cinch, nicely.

She was in fact very well indeed. The trouble was that she had to go on living a normal life at a time when an abnormal one was tapping and muttering in the wings. There was no way of presenting them together, an elephant and a high-wire act. She wanted Aagot all the time. She wanted to come home and find her in bed, and do all her living there with her.

One morning she got up for work, couldn't walk without blundering into chairs and putting her hands against the walls for support. She had a bout of diarrhoea and felt her heart beating like a dying bird. She phoned her doctor and work and went back to bed. While she waited for the doctor to come she made love to herself with a more than usually outrageous phantasy and felt fine. She was warm and had coffee, cigarettes, books and the radio.

The doctor diagnosed a virus infection and gave her a prescription and a diet sheet.

It read:

boiled fish	Lucozade	potatoes
mashed potato	cool milk	white bread
milk puddings	boiled egg	

no coffee	*no* fried foods	*no* cereals
no tea	*no* hot drinks	*no* fruit

Hecka took the scrap of paper to bed with her and read it over like a love letter. She liked the prohibitions especially. Someone cared enough to forbid and underline. She had two happy days in and out of bed, reading, phoning, feverish and content, drinking a lot of hot coffee and eating potato crisps.

She took the rest of the week off work, and because there was a lull in the harsh weather wrapped up and went out for some walks.

One afternoon she stopped walking to watch the children playing at a junior school. The boys shouted and galloped round the playground, kicking a football. Two girls were facing each other. They clapped hands in a complicated patter while they chanted, dipping and pecking:

> See see see my mammy
> Come out and play with me
> Under the app-le tree
> My mammy said to me
> Kiss me
> Cuddle me
> Tell me that you love me

18

> Under the app-le tree
> See see see my mammy
> Come out and play with me . . .

Other girls came over to join in a loose huddle. The patter
was perfect. The teacher on duty noticed them and smiled.
No one organised the ending of the game, there was no end.
It stopped and another began.

> My mother she told me to open the door
>   But I didn't want to
> I opened the door and he fell on the floor
> The dirty old man from China . . .

Hecka looked to see if there were any Chinese children to be
hurt but there weren't.

> My Mother she told me to give him a drink
>   But I didn't want to
> I gave him a drink and he made the glass stink
> The dirty old man from China . . .

They shouted 'But I didn't want to'.

> My mother she told me to take off his hat
>   But I didn't want to
> I took off his hat and it smelled like a rat
> The dirty old man from China . . .

The teacher was watching now.

> My mother she told me to take off his coat
>   But I didn't want to
> I took off his coat and it smelled like a goat
> The dirty old man from China . . .

The clapping pattered and smacked hard.

> My mother she told me to take off his shoes
>   But I didn't want to
> I took off his shoes and he smelled like a booze
> The dirty old man from China . . .

It got faster.

> My mother she told me to take off his socks
>   But I didn't want to
> I took off his socks and he smelled like a fox
> The dirty old man from China . . .

The teacher walked over. The stinks and stripping were too
much for her. She walked, a giant in her sheepskin coat,

among the fly little girls in winter drab. A few scattered.

'Come on, let's play a *proper* game' she said. 'In and out the Dusky Bluebells. Join hands. Alice, hold Tracey's hand. Debbie. Debbie. You never listen. Hold Amina's hand.' Debbie, the loudest singer and least conformable player of proper games, took Amina's hand loosely and let it go.

'Now. In a big circle. Three steps back. And three more. Stop. Janet . . .'

Irritated and enjoying it, the teacher placed Janet where she should be: 'When I say in a circle, I don't mean *in* the circle, I mean . . .'

Semantics wasn't a useful form of attack. 'Right. Sebile, off you go.'

> In and out the dusty bluebells
> In and out the dusty bluebells
> In and out the dusty bluebells
> I – am your master.

Sebile mechanically shuttled in and out.

'Wait a minute. Wait. It's not dusty, it's *dusky* bluebells. Who knows what dusky means?'

Who does?

'It means dirty, miss.'

'No, no. Dusky means, well, dark, shady, in a wood, not very clear, you can't see them because of the trees . . .' The teacher's voice faded. It was a crisis of confidence Hecka was familiar with.

'Anyway. The word is dusky. Let me hear you say it.'

Flattened by obedience, but holding to what they knew to be true, the children reported 'dusty bluebells'. Another word was lurking under.

'For heaven's sake. All right. Let's go on with it.'

> Tippety tappety on your shoulder
> Tippety tappety on your shoulder
> Tippety tappety on your shoulder
> I – am your master.

Tippety tappety spurted naturally from the teacher. Sebile and a friend shuttled grimly.

In and out the dusty bluebells
In and out the dustbin bluebells
In and out the dustbin bluebells

'Stop. Stop.' The under word had surfaced. 'The what bluebells?'

'Dustbin, miss.'

'Dustbin? It doesn't even make sense. Shush. You're like a lot of silly hens. What's a dustbin bluebell? Can anyone tell me?' No one cared to.

'It's dusky. Think how nice that is.'

One or two of the girls looked as if they were trying hard to think how nice that was, or at least to think 'how nice that is.'

'Now. Again. *Properly* this time.'

In and out the dustbin bluebells . . . .

Debbie, Amina, Janet, Tracey, Alice, Sebile trailing a loose shoe; Victory, Victoria, grounded sparrers, clawed at flapping coat tails, loopy dissenters, until the circle collapsed and the old order prevailed. Any pecking to be done they would do.

Hecka went home happy.

*   *   *

June summer evening, Halt Hill, N.W. London, a narrow back garden. Not the roses of Shiraz, the fields of barley and of rye, the essences of Grasse. But mentioned they lie as Aagot ripe with sun on the grass sprawled, belly flat, her hip arched, one leg raising its knee to make a shadow between her thighs, arm looped loose above her head, egg-brown freckles, a ridge of dust along the paler underside. She gazed innocent at the pink and blue of the late day sky, blank beautiful stare which claimed the haze. Could she contrive this, the dark triangle also, the vacuity? It was a great skill, or a great gift. The prehensile naked toes gripping the ground might suggest less than innocence, more than carelessness.

Hecka dipped her hand into the punnet of fruit between them and sucked. She found the darkest berry and brushed Aagot's mouth, the fruit skin breaking and deep red smearing her lips. Aagot startled and lowered her arm suspicious in a swoop to intercept the hand and hold it up, to examine what had touched her.

'Eat it' Hecka said.

'It could have been a worm,' said Aagot. Hecka was scared to front or challenge the implication. As always, it was only later, alone, that such worms flew in the night. She held the moment. A hundred scattered days could pass without another such. She had collected that much sad wisdom.

A full kiss, stooped and sucking, was the only answer to the open lips, to lick away the red juice apology and joy; to unbutton the blue shirt and lay her open, shape and hold her breasts the only response to the arm's gesture; the invitation to peel open the jeans and ease the stalk of the leg to one side.

And it was all impossible, as Aagot must know. A row of back windows, the bedroom look-outs of the normal and married, monitored any illicit taking. Aagot, the plum, the display, was not for picking: and what currency could buy? Hecka, thin, had nothing of value about her person.

Two gardens away, with only low token fences of wire and slats a neighbour woman played and lolled with her spaniel, legitimately stroking, teasing her fingers through its curls, nuzzling and talking and tickling. The dog, by name a bitch, rolled to expose its belly, paws limp, looking with vacant passion at the woman. She pulled its ears, scratched under its throat, tickled in the thin blonde fur of its belly around the nipples, titillating, talking sure love as to a baby, a free lover.

'Provocative little bitch,' said Hecka. Aagot's mouth warmed and widened. She did not blink or turn her gaze and so took the words to heart. Hecka looked up at the sky to see as she saw but even the soft light hurt her eyes.

'I'm just lying here' Aagot said.

'You're always lying here there and everywhere.'

The light gentled and the ground and greens gave the mustered smells of the day. The roses massed their scent, and so the cluster of tobacco plants, the grass grass, the earth as chrysanthemums. Aagot would smell of them all, spiced, the heat of roses, the animal fur. On the line hung limp underclothes, scorched pinks, browns, creams, dying yellows, ochres.

22

The neighbour woman carried her dog on over the threshold limp in her arms. Hecka put her hand on Aagot's belly and held her wrist with the other.

'I must take the clothes in before the dew damps them,' Aagot said, jerked an insect bite, and rose, rose, the touch a sting. A housewife, she unclipped, collecting the pegs in the lap of her shirt and scrunching the clothes into a firm ball. The line stretched bare. It seemed, from experience, that something had been fulfilled, and Aagot would not return from the house. Hecka waited. Aagot returned. She sat.

'Smell,' said Hecka.

'What?'

'The smell. Come to bed now.'

'It's those cats.'

Everyone can choose, everyone who is free. The evening reached its magical turn, brief, when all colours drain except the red and the white. They brazen it until the black takes them. Hecka stared with faulty sight at a low cluster of small white blossom at the end of the garden. She could not remember having seen it before. Alyssum, a rock plant, fresh ground cover? The roses and peonies were blood ripe and known. Hecka muttered some obvious bits of Tennyson. Aagot blinked away the crimson and the white. She yawned.

'What's that white plant over there?' Hecka asked.

'Where?'

'At the very end under the tree.'

'There's no plant there. Nothing grows there.'

'I can see it. White. What is it?'

Aagot got up and picked up and scrunched up the white plastic bag. She went into the house. It seemed, from experience, that something had been fulfilled, and Aagot would not return. She did, to look over the property for other bits of town mess. She found an empty drink can, a piece of broken leather lead, a sweet paper. Hecka shifted uncomfortably, unsure of her ground.

'Yes' Aagot said, 'it's the cats. I believe there's something you can sprinkle on the ground to discourage them.'

'No. Can't you smell the other? The flowers? don't discourage them.'

'Oh, the roses. Yes, a bit.'

Aagot sat. Hecka knew she was keeping her. A brown moth flew. Hecka saw with delight that it settled and pinned Aagot's brown hair. She spoke when she should hold silence.

'I really love you,' she said.

'Oh, love, love,' said Aagot. One arm described a cutting arc to dismiss the tiny word. The moth flew. Hecka lamented her folly. Aagot stood up, stretched, adjusted herself, and tucked the loose shirt into her trousers. She walked to the border and dead-headed.

'Aphids,' she said. 'An awful year for aphids.' She went to the house. It seemed. But she returned with a large metal thing, it looked to Hecka for a moment like a weapon. Aagot walked to the far end of the border and began systematically to pull the handle and press. The reds faded. With each pull breath and sweetness were forced in, with the thrust a grey spray spattered the roses. A chemical filled the air.

Hecka turned her head away, choosing the blindfold. Her fingers grabbed at the threads of grass, she clutched and twisted them, she dug a groove with her nails and finger ends and ran her hands into the earth and stroked. She stooped over the earth and nuzzled the brown soil deep and exposed damp. She filled her face with the grass and sucked it, curling her tongue around the soft leaves to cover her face and sense with the dank and lovely smell. Seeing her coiled so Aagot asked

'What have you found?'

'Nothing,' Hecka said, secret this time, not to be sucked in.

It was ineffective. The hygienic smell of death was strong. Hecka sat with her hands limp between her legs. Aagot came over and looked at the groove and at Hecka's mucky face. Being free, she ignored the eccentricity.

'There,' she said, 'that should finish them off.' She walked into the house. It seemed, from experience, that something had been fulfilled. Aagot did not come out again. The garden was colourless. The lime leaves hung in black rags in the synthesised red town sky.

*   *   *

They were in bed. Aagot snuggled naked, the quilt up to her chin. She had asked for a story. It was a good day.

'Once upon a time,' said Hecka, 'there was a garden with a concrete wall. The wall was made of those pre-cast blocks with holes in them, so you can see in.'

'I know what you mean. They've got those next door,' said Aagot. 'The woman next door said the men who came to build it took ages. And now it's done her dog can get through the holes. It's simply awful.'

'Yes.' said Hecka. 'In the garden behind the wall which was only three feet high and had holes in it so it wasn't a proper wall . . .'

'Why?' said Aagot, 'It's still a wall.'

'Because it doesn't keep anything out and doesn't hide anything away.'

'But it's still a wall. It's *called* a wall.'

'Do you want a story?'

'Well, it's still a wall.'

'Wait a bit and you'll see what I mean by a real wall. The woman made a diamond shaped flower bed in the middle of the garden and sprinkled some National Growmore, then she got some guaranteed glads . . .'

'Guaranteed glads?'

'Yes. That's what caught her fancy too. They grew into tall spikes of Lavender Delight, Golden Haze, Peach Blush and Sunset Glory.'

'Are those real colours?'

'I don't really know. Three of the gladioli were called Sunset Glory. She also planted a sky-blue-pink hydrangea . . . Well?'

'That's not true.'

'Yes it is. We debated it and the vote was yes to the proposition and we looked up and there the sky was, sky-blue-pink.'

'I've never seen anything sky-blue-pink.'

'You've never seen the wine-dark sea or infra-red or heard bat song. Shut up. Are you shut up?'

'Yes.'

'And just for you she planted a Queen Elizabeth rose which

was light pink and extremely hardy and boring and grew to six feet tall. OK?'

'Yes, I've seen them. But you can't say a flower is boring.'

'In fact it was a riot of colour, a real heavy mob. She pulled up bits of grass and sorrel and groundsel and everything else . . . What's the matter?'

'My arm is stuck.'

'Move.'

'I've moved. I've just thought of something.'

'What now?'

'Roses and gladioli don't flower at the same time, I think.'

' . . . She also planted some daffs, large trumpet mixed doubles. And they flowered at the same time. This is a story, OK?'

'But it's not true.'

'No. One summer evening when she was out the back digging up worms for her spaniel . . . well?'

'Nothing.'

' . . . a group of young Crusaders who were collecting for Oxfam knocked at her door. They had a pink plastic sack. She didn't hear them because she was out the back. The young Crusaders looked at her flowers and thought it was an unjust world where one woman had more Sunset Glory than she knew what to do with while other people hadn't a single one to brighten their lives.'

'I don't think that's very nice.'

'Why?'

'It's like making fun of all the poor and hungry people in the world.'

'If you want nice, don't ask me for a story. Anyway, when did you or I last sell all we have and give to the poor?'

'All the same.'

'So they cut off all her flowers and made a big bunch.'

'What about the roses?'

'They brought their secateurs with them. They left a thankyou card and a sliced loaf on her door step.'

'They were collecting for Oxfam and they left her bread?'

'Yes. New high-bake improved something.'

'I don't like that idea.'

'Neither do I. Neither did she. They usually left a handful of rice or a hot cross bun.'

'They'd been before?'

'Yes. She usually gave them a pink plastic bag and they gave her a bun and a thank-you card. She collected them like blood-donation stickers and relics and put them on the mantelshelf. On Good Friday she cried over them. The glazing on the buns liquefied. Or maybe her tears wet them. Anyway, they were tacky that one day.'

'This is silly.'

'Do you want some coffee?'

'No, I don't think so.'

'Shall I go on?'

'I'm getting tired.'

'I'm not. When she saw what had happened to her garden, all those stalks, she was very angry.'

'Why didn't she contact the church and complain?'

'These weren't church crusaders. They were ticket collectors and typists. They moon-lighted as crusaders. They earned a few pennies from heaven on the side. Are you asleep? Anyway, she realised she'd have to build a brick wall, very high, with no holes and a locked gate, and she paid a builder to make it and it cost so much she couldn't afford any gladioli corms or daffodil bulbs and the hydrangeas got hydrangea rot because of the brick dust and the rose got Queen Elizabeth rot because of the cement and in a year her garden was full of ragweed and rosebay and she died and the garden lived happily ever after. Are you asleep?'

'That's the silliest story I ever heard.'

'I know a sillier one.'

'Let's go to sleep.'

'I'm wasted on you. You go to sleep when I talk.'

'That's why you're not wasted.'

'I'm your mogadon? People don't usually go to sleep when I talk. I'm going to be offended.'

'Well do it quietly. I'm going to sleep.'

'Will you dream of sky-blue-pink or hot-cross buns?'

'Neither. I don't dream.'

'What? Why not?'

'There's no point.'

Hecka watches her roll away and curl. She begins to speak in a whisper monotone, wanting to invade such total privacy, her dreamless sleep. She tells the story of an old man who builds a round Folly in his grounds, with a spiral staircase and one round room at the top with one door. As soon as the Folly is completed the door is locked. The old man dies without ever entering the room; the key is buried with him. The ivy climbs the round walls and no-one ever enters the locked room. Aagot sleeps, dreamless. Hecka sits up against the pillows and worries at the empty room.

*   *   *

'What do you feel about me,' Aagot asks. 'Tell me the truth. For once.'

As a confirmed liar then, Hecka was in trouble.

'What kind of truth do you want?'

'There's only one.'

'Could you give me a clue? Is it bible or das kapital? Free range or battery? What does it begin with?'

'What do you feel about me.' The cadence is of a statement not a question.

'Anxious, and as much as I can lay my hands on?' The tone is of a question, not an answer.

'When you're not crude you're incomprehensible.'

'And I thought I was both at the same time. Hell. Which would you like me to be?'

'Neither. The truth isn't in either.'

'That disposes of me as a source of truth.'

*

'Do you love me?' Aagot asks.

'Yes.' The answer comes so prompt upon the question they are both shocked.

'Why? What for?' Aagot asks.

'Yes. I can't say I love you for or because. If I try I know I'm talking mannered nonsense. Yes. So much.'

'You're evading.'

'Yes. I'm stuck like a child who says she loves the house because the chimneys are red, if grown ups keep on at her. The trouble is "because" and "but" and "in" and "on" . . .'

' . . . and on,' says Aagot. 'You talk too much,' says Aagot.

'That's because I can't say anything,' says Hecka.

'Yes you can. You just said something.'

'What? Did I say something?'

'Yes. You said you can't say anything.'

*

'All Cretans are liars, I am a Cretan?'

'You're certainly a liar.'

'When did I last tell you a lie?' Hecka fears it may be mere minutes ago.

'It doesn't matter when. It's not you tell lies sometimes. It's you are a liar.'

'I *am* a liar?'

'Yes.'

'No I'm not.'

'There you are. You are.'

Hecka pauses to cope with the strange implication, then, a test piece: 'The sky is grey . . . ' Aagot looks up to see and Hecka takes fright ' . . . roughly speaking.' Aagot gets up and goes to check. Hecka watches surprised . . . 'is it grey?' she asks.

'Yes.'

'You see, I said it was grey and it is.'

'Yes. But the way you tell it it's a lie.'

'I can turn truth into lies?'

'Yes.'

'How?'

'Things go straight into you and you twist them.'

*

Hecka sits up straight and says 'I am the most truthful woman I know.'

'Ho ho,' says Aagot.

'Yes. That's why I tell so many lies. If I go into the maze to get to the centre I take false turnings and try again. I don't know the way to the middle. Do you?'

'Truth isn't like a maze,' says Aagot.

'What is it like?'

'It's like nothing.'

'Nothing?'

'Yes. It's staring you in the face.'

Hecka puts her hands carefully to the sides of Aagot's face and turns it towards herself to stare into.

*

'I know I love you because I'm so angry with you. That's not why I love. That's how I know I do. You are the whole world. Everything I know and handle and love. But I don't know why. It's not fair to you. I start again with you and try to reach innocence. You are what I most want. If I had you I would understand. I want to be drenched in you and be a slosh of the sea, not a tin can cast up beyond the reach of the tides. But I find myself trying to empty you with my little bucket, dispose of you in muck pools. Please listen.'

Aagot is listening.

'I feel I storm the world when I storm you. You are my hope of redemption. And you are pushing back the intrusions of the world when you check me with a no. Hold me.'

Aagot holds her but does not move towards her. She says.

'You could leave things alone and get on with things.'

'Which? Anyway, I can't. I have to tell the story.'

'There is no story,' says Aagot.

Hecka slips from the embrace. She is frightened.

'There has to be a story,' she says, 'even if it's told by an idiot. It signifies everything.'

'We do what we do,' says Aagot. She is crisp and Hecka knows she does not want this spoken of any more. '. . . There are things to do, ways to behave, a few pleasures. Don't press beyond. It's not safe.'

'How do you know?'

'I do.'

'But *how* do you know?'

30

'I do.'
'You're evading. You can't answer,' Hecka says.

*

"Why did you let me go?
'I didn't. You moved, not me,' Aagot answers.

*

'Tell me the simple truth,' Aagot says.
'For once?'
'Yes.'
'God's in his heaven, all's right with the world.'
'That's not true, that's a story.'
'It's simple enough. How do you know it's not true? If you know what isn't true, you must have some idea what is. You're better at this than I am.'
'I don't want lots of words, just the truth.'
'Oh? Well. I remember there used to be an advertisement in train carriages, in a wooden frame over the seats. It was a picture of a mother and a daughter, and an old man sleeping, sitting in a train compartment, and the girl asks the mother "Why do his teeth go click mummy?" and she says "Because he doesn't use Per-De-Co darling." I thought that was the perfect formula, being able to say "because . . . darling." I used to chant it to myself in hope.'
'In hope of what?'
'That it was the answer. To the question why.'
'What's Per-De-Co?'
'Denture fixative.'
'Do you use it?'
Hecka laughs. 'No.' She is shocked that Aagot implies false teeth free-floating in the universe. For herself, they are still not spoken of and so do, and don't exist. There had been years when she was the only woman who bled although she saw evidence that other women did. No one said. She had been the only woman with sexual desires and extra-arousable parts, although other women around her married and had affaires. They did not speak of it. Other women changed their underwear for some unknown reason: she

31

alone did it because it was soiled.

'Then why don't your teeth go click?'

'That's a good question.'

'So?'

'Don't spoil a good question. I've wasted a lot of my life and spirit trying to say it all holds because of denture fixative. There are a lot more questions than answers, leave them in peace. Don't squash them.'

'Then there's no point.'

'No point in what?'

'Talking. That's what talking is about, getting answers. Otherwise there's no point.'

'Maybe you're right . . . but there are so many points, I can't keep score. They never amount to a heap. I think I resent predictable discourse.'

'But if it's not predictable then it's nonsense.'

'Maybe. But there are so many answers you forget there are questions still lying about. You can't see the flowers for the trees.'

'The *woods*. The *woods* for the trees. And if we didn't accept conclusions without asking questions we'd never move a step.'

'But so many steps and along such predictable paths.'

'The whole point of a path is that it's predictable. It gets you somewhere. Which is more than all this talk is doing.'' Aagot knits, fast.

'Why are you knitting?' Hecka asks.

'Why not? I happen to be knitting, that's all, it doesn't mean anything.'

Hecka is withdrawn, trying to make the denture fixative jingle fit with the rhythm of a train on the tracks. It doesn't. She taps with her nails: click crudeclick incomprehensible clickchildish.

'There can't be more questions than answers,' Aagot says, 'I won't have that. There must be some questions that you ask in the wrong way, that's all.'

'That *I* ask?'

'Yes. If I don't answer a question it's only because I don't know enough fact to answer with, that's all.'

'There are no mysteries, only unsolved problems. Who said that? Is it true?'

'You can't ask that.'

'What?'

'You can't ask that.'

*

'What do you feel about me?' Aagot asks.

'I love you. I want to make love to you, then sleep with you, and make love to you again before you've woken up. When you're away from me and busy I want to watch you and whisper in your ear and fret you and touch you and upset you. I want to intrude on your privacy and interrupt you and make a nuisance of myself.'

'That's not love.'

'No. But I love you while I'm saying it . . . That house over there, opposite, they invited me in once. Their front room is so full of furniture I couldn't live up to it. They've got a kind of sideboard and two layers of carpet and a biscuit barrel with a biscuit packet in it. They shut the windows and drew the blinds and pulled the curtains, they've got both, against the sun. They gave me tea, very weak with lots of sugar and I had to drink it out of politeness and they were very serious and kind and it got hotter in there and I wanted to escape but I couldn't leave because they were so welcoming so I asked if I could see their garden. I was scared that I'd never be able to find my way round all the things in the room. I was turning into a chairback and as I looked I saw there were more things, macramé plant holders with coloured pots in them and plants in them and a glass fruit bowl standing on a glass fruit bowl stand and fruit in it with peel and flesh and stones and pips. They led me out into the garden and it was an oblong of plain grass with high fir trees all round, except the way back into the house, like a grave, a well-kept cemetery.'

'What has that got to do with the truth?'

'I didn't know which I preferred. They were the only choices they gave me; the room or the garden, the impossible or the perfect.'

*

33

Later Aagot lay in bed with the covers kicked down.

'Look at me,' she said. 'For god's sake don't say another word.'

Hecka couldn't say a word.

*   *   *

When Aagot was a little girl she lived in Norway and in England. She spoke two languages. English was used for most conversations of the kind children are engaged in by their parents, that is, instruction and information. They thought they did her a service for life by grounding her in the more international language. Her Norwegian grandparents and cousins, who had less responsibility, joked with her and told her stories in Norwegian.

Somewhere, shut as Rosebud in an attic, she carries the little girl's sense of language. It is not just that she cannot remember how language was a speaking with tongues, the glossolalia of the bush bursting into flames. We all forget that. We must remember that a rose is not a cabbage and we're confounded if we come across a cabbage rose. Worse happened to her. It became necessary that she stay forgetful. When she was still little the language of giants trolls fear mischief bed-time and jokes was suddenly taken from her. Her parents separated and she came to live permanently in England, in a council flat in south London with her mother.

She went to school in England and learned in earnest the language of instruction and information. Her mother was very competent. She was also lonely, fatigued and desperate with her own unhappiness and later with illness. Her sense of responsibility to her daughter grew and it is impossible to joke, talk nonsense or tell a good story from a sense of responsibility. She bought her daughter encyclopaedias.

Aagot went to a good school at some distance from her home, so she did not have the ordinary babble of schoolfriends living in nearby streets. She was not included in those inexplicable bursts of wild laughter over an absurd word or phrase in the classroom, the moments most of us remember when we were free to be hugely silly, to laugh until our stomachs ached and our eyes ran tears and the teacher told us not to be hysterical and we didn't care because for once our nonsense squashed all her sense. Aagot wasn't let in on the joke. It was there to be taken up, but she was not an initiate.

Once, at home, her mother said 'Eat up your cabbage.' She had messed it around a bit and put it to the side of her plate. She said 'Why?' which was strange from a little girl because it questioned a parental order directly and anyway you ate without asking the reason for it. She might more probably have said 'but I don't like cabbage', or worn her mother out by protracted messing, but not 'Why?' Her mother answered 'Because it will make you strong.' Reach out with a good why and a because will tidy you to attention.

Anyway this was an appetising notion. There was a girl at school she would like to check because she kept bumping into her deliberately, giving her a shove, and Aagot wanted to do something to her but didn't know what. She never stumbled when she was bumped because she was always sure-footed, but it annoyed her. She had tried saying 'stop it' with her mother's tone of voice, but it didn't work. The troll-girl ran off laughing. Aagot didn't know any language which would cope with such unreasonable behaviour. She had forgotten it.

So she mushed the cabbage into her potato and swallowed. She gave it half an hour to work, then went out of the flat to the one tree, and tried to push it. Not over you understand, but to make it shift just a bit. She was a believing or literal little girl. She put her shoulder and arm to the tree and shoved. It did not move. She added to her repertoire of understanding that adults told lies. It became her dominant perception of all language which seemed doubtful or silly or likely to incite her into trying to push over trees. It was lies. It was better not to ask arcane questions why. She found a device in the style of adult mimicry to deal with the school shover: one day she said crisply 'you are silly because only babies push' and was never pushed again. Her confidence in prescriptive language increased.

She was lonely. Her mother worked long and hard and did

not see her increasingly correct daughter as a source of conversation, although she herself encouraged the process which made her as she was. The best time of the week was the Saturday outing to the Co-op when she could say the names of the tins and jars under her breath and hope for a small treat; a tin of peach slices, some chocolate spread. She loved sweet things, especially at playtime in school. Her mouth popped and retracted bubble-gum, the other girls burst out rude words. They rhymed and riddled to odd conclusions while she stripped the layers off Allsorts methodically and swallowed them down. From a distance you could think her to be talking with a group of friends, but she was mouthing a toffee, not words.

After school Aagot stood looking out of the flat window at the rain falling on a flat town. When her mother came home from work they spoke minimally of tea and practical problems and she knew that her absence at bed time was a pale pleasure her mother looked forward to. It was a relief when she was not there. Pushed away, she learned to push away. She loved her mother.

This inexplicable support was taken from her too. Her mother became ill and went to the doctor. He prescribed an anti-depressant without examining her. She began to have pains. The doctor, observing a lonely and sad woman, increased the dosage and treated her for nervous dyspepsia and psychosomatic migraine. One day she fell down in tears and pain and Aagot very competently sent for the doctor. He, at last noticing the weight loss and yellowed skin, sent her to the hospital for an examination. After a while and many tests she was diagnosed as having several cancers. Aagot's grandmother came to look after the flat and Aagot, in that order. Aagot was the fruit of the marriage which her grandmother blamed for her daughter's misery. It was not possible for her to love the little girl.

When she returned from school one Friday her grandmother was sitting stiff and formal in the kitchen. Tea was already brewed, a puzzling luxury; usually it waited on her arrival in case the bus was late and the pot got cold and a brew would be wasted. 'Sit down,' her grandmother said. Aagot sat. 'Your mother died this morning. These things happen.'

Aagot had no words to cope with suffering, but she could move, she could always move. She went to her room with decorum and cried, the tears coming from her stomach. She kept as quiet as possible. Perhaps, if she had this once only been allowed; but her grandmother followed her to the room and told her to pull herself together, stop crying, and face the fact that her mother was dead. Simple as being told to put on wellington boots because it was raining, a sensible thing you must do.

She went on crying. Her grandmother, grieved and angry, reminded her that it was worse for her than for Aagot.

'It is worse for me, she was my daughter.'

'But she is my mother.'

'She was my daughter,' said her grandmother, 'But me no Buts.' Strophe and antistrophe: her grandmother's response made her swallow her lament. She kept it down. At the chill funeral the minister said,

'The Lord giveth and the Lord taketh away:
Blessed be the Name of the Lord.'

The injunction to bless and shut up had the last word. Aagot learned, maybe terminally, that there are priorities in suffering, and hers was low. It was better to eliminate suffering. Still, she resented and went on doing so, the claims of others to be injured or bereaved. Passions are not disposable at will. They can be denied but continue to act.

She was ashamed of her mother's death. It was not normal to have a dead mother. She did not want anyone at school to know her distinction. It was doubtful, silly, abnormal as lies; to die. It was not a proper fact. She was already isolated enough. Exhausted by grief she did not go to school on Monday. Lying in bed, her face and head aching with the pain of protracted crying, she worked out a story that her absence had been because of a bang on her head. This had in fact happened five days before, so she was telling a kind of truth which she could believe. A bang on the head gives you a head-ache, with a head-ache you stay home from school. No one can prise open a statement like that and find a darkened room or the question why. It would not leave her open to the contempt, disgust or pity of being a motherless child. Whether her fear was founded on the attitudes of schoolmates or teachers she does not know, but she thought these unmanageable experiences were likely. She was ashamed that her mother was dead. That anyone else should know encroached on the safety of being ordinary.

She told her story in school.

Later she found out that everyone had been told the truth by her grandmother, so they knew she had lied. They had been asked to be 'kind' to her. She did not notice them doing it. She was very angry and dismayed when she discovered that they knew her mother was dead and that she had lied. Her defences against such exposure were strengthened. She learned to speak with silence. Words do not only expend your breath, they spit out blood and tissue. Sweets are kinder. Silence and all such indirect statements give you some control against injury. Better still, to feel as little as possible, so much the less to say, so much less risk of saying it.

She was learning to overcome the feeling of helplessness before the unintelligible. Deprived of playfulness, the right to passionate feeling, and access to the language of art and imagination, she learned that there are simple and effective systems available. You instruct, inform, prescribe, or are silent. Her hope, which she did not recognise as such, was in frightened delight, followed by negation, in the wild and wanton talk of others.

*   *   *

The geography teacher asks,'What's the difference between "peninsula" and "peninsulaR"? What is peninsulaR?'
She writes the two words on the blackboard. Aagot knows, and she knows that the other girls don't, so there is no hurry. She can only gain from keeping silence. She sits at the back of the classroom, where she has the clearest overview, except for that of the teacher. It by-passes the rest of the class.

The teacher lays her head on her arm on her desk in mock despair as the girls chuck mock answers.

'A peninsulaR is when there is more than one peninsula?'

38

'No.'

'So it's when there's just only one peninsula, right?'

'. . . Half a peninsula?'

'A posh way of saying peninsula?'

'A peninsula spelt wrong? You're kidding us?'

'You've been bribed by the Geographical Society to say it's a peninsula, but it's not?'

'. . . It's a peninsula with a man standing on it?'

'It's just a *vision* of a peninsula?'

'. . .Then it must be a peninsula surrounded by land.'

They agree this and assure the teacher that's dealt with: what's the next question?

Aagot says, 'Peninsular is the adjective form derived from the noun peninsula.'

She does not understand jokes. Even the teacher is crushed.

*   *   *

It was a good thing to be a member of the Truth, Dare or Consequences gang. By what recognition they appointed themselves I do not know and they could not have said. It consisted of three or five children, never more or less, never four. If a fourth girl joined, in a few days the challenge would be turned in on her in terms which made her sure to fail and be cast out in total humiliation, abjectness never imposed on outsiders who submitted to the game. If the three approached one and treated her as a familiar, she was being set up. She never knew it. Her face would flush and elation beat high; she would trail with the gang until the awful moment when the trinity would stand around her smiling and say 'Truth Dare or Consequences?' The challenge could not be refused, this was always understood. It was not that you would lose face by refusal, you would not be recognised any more. You would be invisible, unheard, you would sit alone, have no one to talk to or play with. If the three multiplied suddenly into five then number four of the five was safe.

Everyone was sensitive to the coming together, random as it seemed, of the gang in the playground. The game was only played in school time. It needed the constraints of tarmac, walls, warning bells and teachers to flourish and have its virtue. One would be skipping, another giggling across the yard, a third in the toilet. Every movement at playtime was scanned anyway, every fine change in pattern recognised and potent.

Suddenly the three would amble without signal towards one girl. The skipping and talk and giggling went on in the other groups, but sharp focus shifted from the individual centre to the ritual at the edge. The teacher on duty was always unaware of a particular danger. She saw the usual jumble of kids playing. She didn't smell the quickened beat and the fear.

The challenge was given. It seemed very fair: you had after all a generous choice. If Truth, you had to answer truthfully any question the three chose to ask you. Usually it exposed you to shame or mockery. Many shining eyes and acute ears would be ready to challenge you if you tried to act a lie. No one ever did. If Dare: you had to perform any action the three demanded. It was always something risky. You walked the rim of a high wall, you chalked a rude word on the blackboard. If your courage failed and you accepted Consequences the three were free to do whatever they liked to you and usually it hurt.

Dare was the best, if you dared. You came out of it admired. Dare takers often became gang members later. Sometimes the weakest of the triumvirate would retire soon after a particularly good dare and her place be taken by the new heroine. Retirement was sad but not spoken of. You faded, your role remained and was filled. Truth got you laughed at, but if you took it with good humour, even if the baiting lasted for days and gave you a new nick-name as: 'Do you pick your nose?' Yes. 'Snotty. Snotty.': you won the contemptuous affection of all the other victims, it wasn't total loss.

Consequences were usually complete humiliation. Sometimes it was the natural conscientious objector's choice, from a high pitch of courage, but no one ever granted it recognition as that. Choosers of consequences made everyone uneasy.

It was a cruel game, it exposed you to fear and danger. It

was hierarchic. When Hecka played it she always chose Truth. She enjoyed the awful questions and lacked the courage for Dare. When, in her turn, it was played by Aagot's schoolmates, she was never asked. Something about her, her foreignness, excluded her.

It was played by little girls before their retreat from each other at puberty.

* * *

A little girl watches carefully. Then she does what she has been shown to do. She holds her knife and fork so. She eats her greens, her mashed swede. She keeps her mouth closed while she chews. She does not speak with her mouth full. She does not ask to go to the lavatory in the middle of dinner, or leave food uneaten so that she may get to the pudding sooner.

Her nose itches, she has a cold, a lump is at the bottom of a nostril, she picks it out eyes lowered, and then wonders what to do with the cargo under her nail. She slowly moves her hand towards the under rim of the table.

She knows she will be observed. She is. She knows she will be told she is disgusting. She is told. She knows she is disgusting. She doesn't think how nice it would be to get away with something. That idea doesn't get a chance until she is about thirty years old. At thirty she regrets the years wasted in pursuit of approval.

The fact that in the interval she has learned to use a handkerchief is no big deal.

*

A little girl is cornered in the playground by girls no bigger than she, but singular in being fearless among the fearful. They are small queens, imperious. An imperatrix with red hair asks,

'Are you a P.L.P.?'

'What's a P.L.P.?'

'Don't ask questions,' says Trixie, 'Just say yes or no: are you a P.L.P.?'

No seems safer, it usually is.

'No, I'm not.'

'Then you're not a Proper Living Person.'

A little madam with brass brown eyes asks again,

'Are you a P.L.P.?'

This time: 'Yes, I am.'

'Then you're a Public Leaning Post,' says Maizie.

The little girl does not know that you can refuse the terms of a question.

The fact that she learns to play the same game is no big deal.

*　　　　*　　　　*

All speaking of passion, possession, deceit, myth, art and artifice, wickedness and redemption, deviousness, and the meaning of gesture, were urgently shifted by Aagot into practical and resolvable issues. Passion and possession are distortions of love and love is an exaggeration for friendship. Deceit, artifice, deviousness, in so far as they are not paranoid delusions, are misunderstandings by the receiver, in Hecka's case obtuse misunderstanding of simple truth and integrity. Wickedness does not exist. Myth is pre-scientific thinking. Gesture is movement of the body, and the body simply moves. If the body crashes out the door, it is the door which simply crashes, the body having moved it with a certain velocity and vigour. Art does not exist, or will not until women make an acceptable one in consensus workshops. Life is simple, truth is staring you in the face. The iron ferocity, the urgency of these clipped dicta made Hecka shiver with real cold and fright. Lacking sensitivity she took these statements of the non-existence of so much she lived by, their absence or nonsense, as statements that they did not exist for Aagot. She took the ferocity to be righteousness and right-thinking. She forgot that privacy has many facets and holds in many desires, not all of which can be crashed into even by gesture, or movement of the body. Later she began to understand, when it was too late to do anything about it. Too late was the only possible time to understand, just as the only possible time for dialogue to begin can be after one of

42

two has died and the relict of the above knows for sure there is not infinite time to talk in, and the dead would know that even more surely, if she could know anything. Hecka was free to invade only when all spoils were beyond her taking.

She began to speak in her sleep to Aagot, forcing announcements on her and breaking into her rest. It was all over in a moment and usually forgotten by them both when morning came. Once Hecka saw the words she had been jumbling around in conscious talk, written in white chalk capitals refined to one word on a blackboard. She turned to Aagot in the dark and explained ' . . . Cavity. It's Cavity.' 'What?' But Hecka had already forgotten.

*   *   *

3. The Whole Point

Only two things matter; ecstasy and truth. I am frightened that they deny each other.

'Spaniels are nice,' said Mrs. Hibbert, still knitting. 'Silky ears. I'd have a spaniel.'

Mr. Hibbert nosed up from his cup, looked at the TV to see if there was a picture of a dog, then down without words. She's doing it again. Still, the house is clean. Keeps herself neat, her stockings don't sag, sure sign that in a woman. Doesn't show me up in public yet.

The TV documentary on one-parent families ignored her. It had nothing to do with spaniels. Neither did he, nor, as far as he knew, did she. 'Yes,' she said, 'much better'. Better than what, for Christ's sake; cats, budgies, him?

He used to think she did it because it pertained to something he'd missed and he'd say 'What?' and she'd look puzzled; then that she spoke out of a day dream and he was offended by the exclusion. That was in the days when they used to speak when spoken to. Then that she did it to annoy. Now he understood. At fifty nine she was becoming a bit queer in the head, senile. Childish nonsense. Thank God he was still compos mentis, thank God. With a bit of luck that would be her bit for tonight. Spaniels were a new one. His irritation was numb: mild affliction was a comfort.

He watched with distaste as a disorderly woman on the screen whined about the problems of managing on benefits. Shouldn't have kids, shouldn't live so messy, that's the whole point, look at that, smoking, her hair looked dirty.

Nose up again. Mrs. Hibbert's hair was close permed, tinted warm brown. Her hands never fluttered distraught through her hair, or pulled on a filthy cigarette, she didn't whine. Self respect, that's the whole point.

Jesus, sweet lord, give me less pain or more so that I know. Don't leave me here. I hurt but not enough to understand. What is it? So slow, each stitch. I knit very even, Lily said, each stitch a word, in a row, making a pattern the same as the last row until it is finished. How many scarves? Plain. I am always sensible. Plain but sensible. It always makes sense. Finally a useful scarf for Ed. How could they? Sweet lord, you gave yourself to them so they could hurt you to the pain of death. Didn't you know? You knew. Help me, dear Jesus sweet, tell me, you died so young, I am numb with too much age. They say you live, visit me, speak to my

47

wounds, open them with your gentle hands, pick me open, unpick me let me bleed, at least. Enough is not enough.

Her lips are moving. That's because she's counting stitches. That's all right. All women do that. That's not madness.

I have washed up. I have kept myself clean. I do not know the world, my lord. I do not even know the people I know. I know my house. I know my garden which has peace roses and a lawn without weeds. Do you tell only those who already know, the important men? Do you tell in the offices and the churches? I am too small in my chair and my walls. Should I have walked out into the wilderness; have you left me for the wilds? Perhaps I am too mean. I am too mean. I have valued my comfort above all, balmed my wounds before they could speak to me, but they ache with voices, Jesus, make me hear what they say. But the little dog. The animals? For a moment when Lily was born, no, not Lily, in that pain, drenched, it seemed: but the nurses talked and gave me injections and I was sensible again. Perhaps in the sea below all. I would be tossed, saturated a sponge, flooded my mouth eyes nose ears then lungs stomach intestines. I would have to fight against the loss, the change, I would cling to a piece of wood and so I would not know. You walked in hot deserts and hurting sun and were thirsty for water. I go to the shops, my feet ache, I need cups of tea. I am soft but I hurt. It is not enough. 'More tea?'

'I wouldn't mind. Do you want this on?'

'I don't mind.'

'It's getting nippy.'

'Yes'.

'Will it be done soon?'

'Not long.'

'Good.'

'Tea or coffee?'

'Too late for coffee.'

'Do you really like this grey?'

'It's all right.'

A row finished. Needles pushed through the ball. Mr. Hibbert watched TV alone. It was better. Her chair was empty. When she dies he will be eased. He can care for the house. A man on the TV was talking confidently of the emotional strain of being a mother and father to his children.

Mr. Hibbert could hoover. There is a washing machine. He would remove the photos of Lily on the sideboard. They belong to her. He would put in the bin the plaster statue of Christ exposing a round red stylised heart. Lily should have known better than to encourage her. He could shop and wash up and make the bed. To sleep alone would be good. But there is the ball of grey wool and the needles. She always leaves some reminder, never clears out completely, always leaves some trace. How pleasant it would be to go to British Home Stores and pick a ready made scarf or jumper. No tape measures over the shoulders and across the outstretched arms.

Mrs Hibbert brought in a tray with two cups of tea on saucers. She stirred his. He could do that.

'Did you read Lily's letter?' she asked.

'No.'

She sat in her armchair. She counted the rows of plain. It was time to refer to the pattern.

'Getting Late.'

'Yes.'

'I'll have this in bed.'

'I'll just do this bit.'

Help me, help me. I have waited all these years. Tell me what to do. Two together. If I could be your mother. You would talk to me. I would offer you food and flasks of tea when you went for days into thirsty places. You would say no and explain to me why. I would bathe you and give you warm towels and welcome your friends and listen and then I would know why the comforts are not enough. Then you would love me. Pearl. I would knit for you anything you asked, the most difficult of patterns, and socks for your feet with turned heels. If I take more pains, perhaps. I shall sit up tonight and finish this. My fingers ache now. My eyes are tired. I will stay up and finish. Then. And press it. Then. If I make fringes too, if I try hard all night. Come now, now, I have never needed you so much. My body aches as it did in the days when I bled. I know you are alive, I saw you this morning, you showed me you are here, the little spaniel body, you screamed to me as I stepped into the road to tell me, you died just in front of me, you prevented me. I saw your pain beyond belief, the car moved faster then, everything moved on faster but you stayed and looked

49

at me. I am trying, help me, tell me if I am doing wrong, tell me what other to do. It is not enough that I am doing what I can. The house is clean. This is not good enough, the grey, the plain, it is too easy. Mother said: she is a hard-working girl, not much spirit perhaps, but diligent. If I make bands in that hard pattern, can I remember? I can make myself; and other colours and patterns, beautiful. If I start again and do better. The sound of the needles is too easy, one grey thread is too simple, I know more.

Mrs Hibbert pulled her plump self out of the armchair and fetched the tapestry bag in which she kept the odd left over balls, old skeins, from the jackets, bootees, woollies, socks, bed-jackets, twin-sets; years of experience pushed down into the bag too small for them, each one separate though, the wool end carefully twisted around itself to stop the unravelling and mixing which she knew happens to all untended things, left to themselves. She opened the mouth of the bag by its cane handles and began to pick out with gentle fingers, to see what she had.

What is it that has been done? The little dog died and I stood still and put my shopping bag on the pavement and it tipped over and the tomatoes and a tin rolled out and the cars went on just the same and the people walked by us just the same: no, two young people laughed as they walked by, and I saw Lily going as she went before. And it was not so, not my shopping list, my list of tasks, not a list at all, but all telling me one name. I do not understand. What is it that has been done?

The yellow angora in crowds strong as mimosa and all frail flowers, yellow heads hanging daffodil and crocus, slashed by the rain, yellow flesh pieced out by sharp bird beaks, all incomplete, dark cold rods of sleet, the heavy grey fisherman's knit, splashing them with spots of brown mud, row after row it falls on them injuring and spoiling while it wets their ground, as tears and blood and wetness are needed.

Fingers held the yellow, the grey, the brown, searched skilfully for the matt linen thread as cog wheels formed in black space of all colours, wheels which meshed then missed. One spun off, born faulty, teeth broken, unable to grip, waited alone in the black for the age, still, when its partner, its match and mate, would surely come.

50

Across the centre a gash of red held by black silk sutures which pull the wound painfully against the weight of the fabric.

It was time for the Epilogue. Middle-aged men and women sang. The colour had gone out of adjustment again, the red was rayed from the poinsettias at the altar, it crossed the lilies with red lacerations. Faces and voices empty of anything except earnestness were singing.

> Hasten the day, hasten the day,
> The Day that shall surely be
> When the earth shall be filled with the Glory of God
> As the waters cover the sea . . .

I have seen the sea, many times. I have stood on the shore and looked across and known that there is surely out of sight but surely a farther shore, and others enclosing the sea at the sides. But the Waters? Where are They? I have never seen the Waters. I have seen the earth, but not the waters, nor the glory of god.

The needles moved with no common sense. Lily was there too, and Ed, Lily a crown with the stones missing, holes waiting to be filled, Ed a band of quiet blue with small repeated ticks of orange edge to edge; herself too, a cat's cradle mesh full of ways in and ways out, no centre, random runnels leading back to and out from her corner, loose, open, graceless in form. *In everything that matters I have no choice. Only in things not worth the choosing can I choose. In everything that matters I must understand, try not to leave out and lie.* Her fingers check that no back thread has been lost.

At the end she gathered all the colours, all the threads, and wove them so that they were all used, everything she had and so could know, flecked and darted them into the design so they clustered and informed.

She slipped into bed, unconscious and irresponsible as after birth. Ed stirred.

'I finished it,' she said.

'What?'

'It is finished.'

She dreamed of the little dog, that she held it as it died, sweeter on her breast than any baby, and that it looked brown-eyed at her, and comforted her as it died. Its body

51

flat open a bloody mass against her. It clothed and altered her.

In the grey and normal morning he rose and made tea, then went into the sitting room to pull the curtains. The thing was lying all over the armchair, a big gaudy rag. He held the thing up. Damned great holes, what are the damned holes for? You can't wear a garment full of bloody great holes. The whole point is. Clothes clothe you, don't let the cold in, don't expose you. Unless its some flimsy fancy girls dance in. He feels insult rising at her madness, at the form it takes. Who does she think he is? But that's the whole point, she isn't thinking of him any more. She sits and knits and talks and keeps his house clean, but inside she's going soft, shapeless, and makes this mess, this nothing, can't be worn. He turns the swathe of fabric in his hands. It's not a scarf, not a jumper, a cardigan, big as a blanket but no use, big as a bedspread, but who could sleep under that tattered; what's it for? No nameable shape. A bloody mess.

She slept sweet, not knowing that providently from affection to save her, he was trying to unravel what she had done so no one would witness it, not even she when she woke.

What he did not see was the back of the making, where the threads were left at the end of a statement but not cut off, each one taken up again to be part of a star, a flower, a knot, a bruise, appearing from the front as a speck, a comma, a large nameable section, a band, a broken stripe of purple or gold, from the back, the unseen side, always present, never past or abandoned, sometimes reaching suddenly up to join in again, the web's making, the concealed working, what she did, what made one piece of utter differences.

*   *   *

Lily pointed to an old woman in a corner chair.

'Talk to her. Mrs. Harris. I'll be off in fifteen minutes.'

Everyone else in the ward looked at Hecka, only Mrs. Harris had her head down. Hecka put her trust in Lily's perversity in directing her to the only patient who looked indifferent to being visited. Perhaps the old woman was asleep. Hecka sat down on the edge of a low table. The old woman was so small that Hecka, sitting, still looked down at the crown of her head, at the thin white hair.

She looked round for Lily. She was taking the weight of a very fat woman walking to the door. Lily waited for the woman to make slight movements forward on thick ankles and dragging feet. Lily took the strain and followed on. She was talking quietly and the woman nodded a sullen head. Hecka turned back with suspicious trust to her task.

'Mrs Harris?'

The old woman looked up and smiled.

'May. You've come.'

There was joy. Hecka couldn't cope.

'No. My name is Hecka. I'am a friend of Lily's.'

'Lily?'

'Hecka, a friend of Lily. You know Lily?'

The old woman was confused. She looked beyond Hecka at the walls and other patients as at a strange place she suddenly found herself in from a more probable one. Her grey eyes had a visible milk of cataract hiding her own vision. She looked towards Hecka.

'May. You've come. How is Vicky?'

'Fine.'

'And Vicky, how is she?'

'She's fine, and how are you?'

'I'm tired of this place. These people. How's mother? And Dad?'

'They're fine.'

They must have died decades ago, Hecka thought.

'And May?'

'I'm May,' said Hecka, for her own sake.

'There's one thing I'll say, this place is clean. Mother always kept the house spotless. Spotless. And Dad such a clean man. Yes.'

'Yes,' said Hecka.

'Yes. She took prizes for it. A lovely figure. Being a dancer. Such tiny feet. Size ones.'

She moved her hands to cup the shape of a mere lotus and smiled at the place between her hands.

'Your feet are small,' said Hecka prosaic, 'about size three, aren't they?'

'Yes, size one she takes. Dancing all the time. In the house. While she was working. A lovely figure. She took prizes for it. How's mother?'

'She's well,' said Hecka, 'Still dances.'

'Dances? Oh, yes.'

Hecka, half behind the curtained eyes, half audience, made a critic's error.

'Were you happy when you were a child?'

'A child?'

She saw it didn't matter. The old woman was shielded by a blaze of lights, stage and age-blind, from any harm Hecka could do. As Hecka looked she saw the brightness fading.

'Mother is well,' she said quickly.

'How many of us are there?'

'Ah. Well. There's you. Who else is there?'

'There's Tom. And Vicky. And May.'

'Yes.'

'And Tom of course.'

'Yes.'

'Have you seen Tom lately?'

Hecka was happy.

'No. I haven't seen him for a while.'

'Yes. Spotless. And clean clothes for us all on Sundays with Dad being a tailor. Always well turned out. Never touched a drop. He said "I'm not a teetotaller." No. Only Christmas he'd have a glass of port with mother. Have you seen mother lately?'

'No not for a while.'

'A fine tailor. All the gentry came. The queen came. Everyone knew him. He was proud of her when they walked out. A lovely figure. Being a dancer. A little waist like that.'

Her fingers span a small circle and she smiles at the place.

'Lovely hair. It just grew in ringlets. She didn't have to curl it. She brushed it and it made ringlets. He was proud of her. She danced for the queen.'

Victoria, thought Hecka.

'Yes. Treated them well. Gave them presents for the

children, little presents. Treated the women well, being a socialist. Time off when they needed it.'

'He was a socialist?'

'Yes, a strong socialist, always going to meetings.'

'Did he go to church?'

'No, he's not a believer. But a good man. Sent us to Sunday School.'

Hecka understood why Lily sent her to Mrs. Harris while other patients looked out for visitors. The old woman needed only to look in, with a witness, and her world was peopled, the text written, the elements immutable as a mass. Hecka had only to say the right words, to say them again, not vary or innovate, and her world, no more esoteric than any other, was renewed, filled and flawless. To name their names was enough for them to appear, Victorian Edwardian, orderly, fair-dealing, clean, dancing, curly, kind, loving, made perfect: Mother, Dad, Tom, Vicky, May. What could the old woman have been or done to make such a heaven? If I am left just one, perhaps, thought Hecka; but there has to be me for there to be one other and it will not happen. I shall scratch and claw and make hell.

Lily came.

'So May is here.'

'Yes. I knew she'd come. Where's Vicky and Tom?'

'They come. You know. Look, I've got this lavender water for you. Smell.'

She put some on a tissue and smoothed the old woman's wrists and forehead.

'I remember that smell . . .' Hecka began.

'Yes. Now and then. Rest now, Mrs. Harris, until May comes again, then you'll be ready for her. She'll come soon.'

The old woman leaned back and dropped her head.

'Haven't got long,' said Lily as they walked out, 'He rang. Mrs. Hibbert's not well. I'm going over.'

'Time for a coffee?'

'We'll have it in the kitchen.'

While Lily boiled the kettle Hecka asked

'Was her mother really a dancer?'

'Really? I suppose so.'

'And her father a tailor, a socialist?'

'Don't ask me, ask her. She knows.'

'Did he make clothes for the queen?'

'He does now.'

'Dead?'

'Of course. Long ago.'

'And May, how did you know I was May?'

'Because May always comes.'

'Other visitors you mean?'

'Yes. Anyone. May comes.'

'Vicky? And Tom?'

'Vicky her sister. Dead. Tom died at Paschendael.'

'All dead. Is she dying?'

'Yes. No. When they die she die. Or they all live. When she begins to forget them then I know she's going.'

'Was she always so sweet?'

'No, she was difficult. Her children tell me so.'

'There's hope then. For me, there's hope.'

Lily's eyes narrowed.

'There's grace. Unless you reckon to sweeten up very sudden.'

*   *   *

Lily let herself in.

'Still kept your own key, I see,' said Mr Hibbert.

'Yes. What's the matter with her?'

He refused to look up.

'You're the nurse, not me.'

'You've sent me for a diagnosis? If she's ill, why didn't you get the doctor?'

Lily returned home to her foster parents without a trace of West Indian speech. She had learned years ago that the change of language made him know she withheld herself.

'Why? Why? I'll show you why.'

His mouth was dried and pulled out of shape. The beads of spit in the corner of his mouth, his blundering walk to the front room, would melt any softer heart than Lily's. He was an old man. Clothes which had fitted him in his middle years hung awkwardly from his body, the trouser legs twenty years the wrong length, the jacket out of true from his way of raising one shoulder, the V of an old sweater knitted by his wife twisted to the left by the warp of his gestures. Lily was unmoved. He indicated the mass on the chair without looking at it.

'Look. This is what I found this morning. This. And how do you explain this?'

She ignored his accusation of responsibility for whatever it was. The worst of it was she was not wounded by his disgust. He pressed: 'I haven't had my dinner today, only stuff out of tins.'

Lily held up the fabric. She is small, and holding it up wide concealed her completely except where the red gash hung open held by black threads. The small centre of her body in a belted grey coat showed through. The stuff was wild with the threads he had tried to pull and unwind. They gripped in knots he had forced trying to make them unlock. The more violently he had pulled the more they had tightened and the stuff was puckered and distorted, to his eyes no worse than when she had left it for him to find. The band of blue and orange remained neat. He could not find the threads for it laced into the back.

He was no knitter, and despising the flimsy nature of things made by women, the cups of tea, hot dinners, garments, he had been surprised that the piece of soft stuff, big and repulsive as it was, had refused to come apart in his hands.

One way he cared for her was with tenderness for her soft body which, he felt, would suffer and be broken more, and more easily; and with tender contempt for the things she worked to make, the food he ate, the warmth and softness and variety with which she padded the stone and brick of his frame and his house. When he was angry he knew how to shake her by making a mess of the food she put on his plate and then leaving it, dropping separated sheets of newspaper on the floor, slopping his tea or leaving the back door open so the cold invaded the warmth she made. It had been very easy to do.

Once, in the early days of their marriage, being awed by her femininity, he had fancied slapping her carefully made-up face to leave a red mark and bring water to her eyes so the mascara would run, pulling her head by its permed and set hair to destroy in a few moments the decoration she had taken hours to present to him. It would have been easy. He never did it. Neither did he ever learn it is possible as an act of love to handle curls, words, paint, soft and tearable stuff, to play with them and set them gently aside until he uncovered the creatrix.

He had managed to keep his eyes off the plaster Jesus these years and to blame Lily for it. Now his wife returned his respect and tolerance with a nonsense about dogs, no reason in it, and with a mis-shapen parody of all the quiet and careful things she had ever made. She lay in bed in the day-time, ignoring him in affected or abnormal sleep, it didn't matter which. She ignored him. His hurt was deep.

'How is she?' Lily said. She put the stuff carefully on the chair.

'Last night. I went to bed and she was making a scarf. She was talking to herself. That surprises you. You didn't know about that. I have to put up with that. She came to bed late talking some nonsense and when I came down in the morning here it was.'

'Have you asked her what it is?'

'Me? I have to live with this all the time. It's for her to explain to me, not me to go begging her for words. You're the one who understands everything. You tell me.'

'Where is she?'

'In bed. Still sleeping.'

Lily walked through to the kitchen to put a kettle on to make tea to take upstairs. While it boiled she came back to the front room and laid the knitting on the floor, pressing parts out to see clearly. Ed went into the kitchen. He was avoiding her. It was growing dark. She took off her coat and walked in her grey uniform dress to the kitchen for the tea pot and cups. She switched the light on. Ed sat at the table with one hand across his eyes. There was wet between his fingers and his mouth dribbled.

'Who are you crying for?' she asked coldly. She walked to

the door with a loaded tray and bottle of tablets she'd brought with her.

'Where's my tea?'

'There's still hot water in the kettle.'

'If you're staying for supper, I don't know what you can make us. She hasn't been to the shops.'

'You don't do yourself justice.'

Lily took the tray upstairs.

'Mrs Hibbert.'

At the sound of Lily's voice she woke. Ed had been up three times to stir her but she hadn't woken.

'Here I am. Tea.'

'Lily. Lily. What time is it?'

'Never mind.'

'Let me tell you . . .'

'Yes. And tea. And in return give me what you made.'

'What I made? Oh, yes. It's coming, Lily. You smell of lavender. It's for you.'

A door slammed and there was a crash and two thuds from downstairs. Mrs. Hibbert sat up and reached for her neat bedjacket.

'It's all right,' said Lily. 'It's only Ed breaking the statue. He's wanted to for years. Let him.' She laughed. Mrs. Hibbert began to cry.

'Why?'

'Don't worry. He always hated it because I gave it you and he never understood. He meant no harm to you. I'll get you another. There are as many gods as you could ever want.'

*   *   *

Hecka grieved as if loss had happened if there was no meeting, no words, sometimes for as little as a few hours; this time she must have gone. So strong was her belief that the loss of love must happen. If it's beautiful it's going to leave you, she had learned, recited, set herself as an imposition, traced the consequences of that belief all her life, found evidence of its truth all her life as we can find evidence of any belief, it is a matter of the choosing or the initial shove in one direction.

It was not tolerable to Aagot, nor would it be to anyone loved or loving. It was a way to avoid pain by substituting another more bearable. Hecka loved courage most of all, because she did not have it. Next to courage she admired stoicism, because she did. She lived on second best. It was easier and she knew its workings.

She tried to explain to Lily, who listened with narrowed eyes as they walked from the hospital, and said 'What happen to you: an acorn fall on your head?'

Hecka was angry this time.

'I have my sky too,' she said.

'Yes, I'm sorry,' said Lily, not looking at her. 'I'm ashamed.'

They walked on in the rain.

'Lily, tell me about your father and mother.'

'Why do you ask?'

'Because I don't know much about you.'

'Why now? Anyway, you never will . . .'

Truth time again, Hecka thought. Lily handed the small umbrella to her. Hecka got soaked very quickly even in small rain. It didn't penetrate Lily's dense brown hair but held in small shining drops. The shoulders of her mac darkened, that was all.

' . . . It's not important,' Lily said, 'You're fire and I'm water, that's all.'

'Astrology?' said Hecka, incredulous.

'What? No. You are small fire and I would quench you.'

They walked on scheming in silence.

'I could take a matchstick to you, boil you away,' Hecka said.

'You ever hear of a river dried up by a matchstick? Huh.'

All the same, Hecka was glossy with rain and satisfaction.

'You don't reckon much to me, do you. What about my pure clear light, little candle burning in the night?'

Lily shrugged her thin shoulders. She never touches me, Hecka thought, but all the time she smooths me.

'Yes I do,' said Lily, 'you burn good. All right. I don't know my father. My mother had hard times and fostered me to Mrs. Hibbert when I was three. Mrs. Hibbert had a baby girl who died. She took to me, whatever the neighbours say. My mother take me back when she can. She had another baby when I was seven and I didn't see her again.'

Hecka flicked rapidly through notions of Between Two Cultures, Deprivation of Mothering, Identity Crisis, and she shut up.

'Any wiser?' Lily asked.

'Who did you love?'

'Do. Mrs. Hibbert.'

'But you call her Mrs. Hibbert, not mother?'

'She asked it. I was fostered. She was sparing all three of us.'

'But she mothered you.'

'Yes and I have a mother. I came from a womb. Like you. Mother isn't just change the nappies and be kind, whatever the book say. My mother grew me and bore me. Maybe they don't like to think on that too much. They prefer it a man or a machine can be a mother. Then no problem for them; no mystery.'

'Them?'

'Them.'

'But you love Mrs. Hibbert.'

'Yes. But my mother my mother just the same.'

'Is she alive?'

'I don't know.'

*   *   *

The hospital ward was decorated for a Christmas party. Balloons, tinsel, paper chains, holly, a very few Christmas cards, a silent record player. It was the same every year.

Hecka came early to help. Lily tested her immediately by telling her to sit in the dining area and wait, she would only be in the way. As usual, she took the trial well. She ritually protested and was ignored. She left her offering of a bottle of port in the kitchen and went to sit down. She was sore and tired as always around Christmas and this year was under-weight and had times of crying and shaking. Being near Lily gave her a rest, which was not what Lily intended. Often Lily looked irritable at the signs of Hecka's face relaxing, the flicker being wiped away. Hecka could stop aiming at things for a while, which was a relief because she didn't know what she was supposed to aim for. Lily told her what to do and she lost nothing.

Lily didn't often look at Hecka but when she did it was with eyes narrowed. Hecka wondered if saints and healers grew irritable with the immanence of the wounded, sinners, the merely inept, expecting to be blessed, healed, and given a piece to take away. She knew they were wearied by giving: the power went out of them, she remembered.

She sat and gawped. A cut-out Father Christmas on the wall was presenting a big gold parcel to a child. It's hands reached out tentatively. Santa's sack was still bulging full of things to give. He looked red and fat, not at all depleted. But he had gnomes on the production line at the North Pole, and inexhaustible reindeer, and his very own sledge. He delegated. He was a benevolent corporation. He was a man. He got the thank-you letters.

Facing her was a painting of a mother and baby, a permanent picture in the ward. A Madonna it must be, of course, Hecka thought; I'm not well, my mind is blurred, I saw it as just a mother. The mother looked pale and concentrated on the fat boy child, her breasts covered but defined as full of milk, her fingers white and limp, the baby's fingers grabbing towards her. Behind was a landscape of yellow fields and trees. She could not turn to look, her eyes were trained on the child. She was fixed. Her lap was there to be sat on, her full breasts must be available to be drained by his urgent mouth. Hecka, paramenstrual, was caught by the image. The cost of being in the foreground seemed rather high.

The Madonna sat the Infant firmly on his bottom on the ground; in one gesture she pulled the blue veil off her head and shook out her squashed brown hair; lifted up her skirts, turned her back on child and looker, walked firmly away into the field, bottom swinging, picking handfuls of preserved wildflowers, heartsease, cowslips, tossing them into the air, singing stridently. The infant screamed with rage and fear as its fingers grabbed nothing, its mouth sucked cold air. With Hecka it looked at a desolation of random specks in darkness, impossible to fathom or make sense of, no temperature now, no touch, no pattern, attributes of any kind: indifference. Hecka knew and she was shaking.

Lily put her head out of the kitchen door.

'What are you staring at? You want a drink?'

'Yes please.'

Lily didn't ask what kind of drink. Not port, thought Hecka, port is what I give, not what I like to get. She looked at the balloons full of air but tethered in stagnant bunches to the walls. No breeze to play with the paper chains and make them riffle. The evergreens, neither alive nor dead, hung in isolated bits. It was a bad year for berries. The tinsel had had shinier years. The patients sat in the sitting room, she saw them through the glass panels, in clean crimplene for Christmas. She could just see Mrs. Harris, small as a child, her head dropped, and the woman she thought of as Fat Edna staring an angry blank across the room.

Lily brought out a plastic tumbler one third full. Hecka hoped it wasn't some sweet Christmas special.

'Ta.' She tasted. It was neat whisky.

'Suit you?'

'Yes. Ta.'

Lily's eyes narrowed to her smile.

'I hope you are ready to play some games.'

'I can't play games. I never could.'

'Then you're starting late.'

Hecka helped to carry out plates of battenberg, sponge, iced fancies, crisps, sausage rolls, sandwiches, between gulps of whisky. Games, oh Lord she never could remember the rules. She moved chairs into place. Looking aside at the patients, she saw they hadn't moved. They could be glass paintings on the door panels. Smash a pane and there would be flecked darkness behind. She was still shaking a little though the whisky helped. It surprised her that her thinness was being taken up by the world; things were thin, and this in the middle of a festival solid with repeats.

'Lily.'

'Don't worry.'

'What kind of games?'

'This is a hospital.'

The party began on an instant, no introit or warming up. The nurses walked into the sitting room together, a Friend of the Hospital sat at the piano and struck three summoning chords, then played some emotional numbers, 'Nellie Dean', 'If You Were the Only Girl in the World', 'There's a Long Long Road...'. Some nurses sang, others smiled. The patients remained so. One was coerced to her feet to dance a few steps to 'Sweethearts, Sweethearts', with a nurse. Hecka wondered why they didn't bring in some drinks. The ward cat was fondled and stroked. Nothing was asked of anyone except that they enjoy themselves. Only that. 'I'm dreaming of a White Christmas' became 'Once in Royal David's City'. The singing wasn't catchy and the gloom deepened. Hecka felt a rigid smile on her face.

In 'While Shepherds Watched' Fat Edna began to swear, slow and loud. Her face was red and her gaze on the middle of the room so the attack was general and particular to each.

'Fucking sheep shit, ...baa ...baa ...'

The nurses stopped their light conversation. Fat Edna's thighs and bosom were enormous.

'All seated on the ground...'

'Fat arse-holes... what's between your legs?'

'The angel of the Lord came down,'

'One screw and you've forgotten what it's for...'

'And glory shone around.'

'Shrivelled old twats, no juice out of you, poke and piss...'

The prudent pianist finished on a chord. Lily walked over to Fat Edna.

'Piss off you' said Edna.

'You know, don't you,' said Lily.

Edna's cry of 'Yes...' was shocking. It went on as long as her breath could last to make it. It was a shout of triumph and grief, one. She grew bigger as the cry left her.

'Yes, you know,' and Lily got up and walked away.

Hecka and all waited for more, for explanation, but nothing.

'Blind Man's Buff,' said a nurse. They moved the small table from the centre of the room. The walking patients and the few visitors stood, hoping to lurch into a party.

'Get up,' said Lily.

'I've sprained my ankle,' said Hecka.

'Shall I strap it up for you?' said Lily.

'I'll get up.'

'Everybody in a circle.'

It was required that the circle be perfect in roundness and spacing. Wheelchair patients, including Mrs. Harris, were pushed into place. The empty space in the ring looked vast. Once it was formed, who would dare cross it? Lily, elected, stood in the dead centre. Her eyes were bound with a black scarf. A nurse turned her three times and stepped backwards out of the circle. Someone started the record player with tunes dated but not nostalgic.

> Where has your momma gone?
> Where's your momma gone.
> Where has your poppa gone?
> Where's your poppa gone.
> Far, far away . . .

Lily went on turning in her small centre, increasing speed. The black band became a circular blur with no knot, a blindness demonstrated. She stopped dead without swaying. She was at ease in darkness.

> Last night I heard my momma singing this song
> Ooh-ee, chirpy chirpy cheep-cheep
> Woke up this morning and my momma was gone . . .

She began to move in an unwind from the centre, slow, grave as a ceremonial dancer. Everyone was entranced watching her arms lift slowly, marking her passage through the outward movement, not stumbling, her palms turning to push back the space she had covered. She was so sure, the unwinding could be endless, the circle her territory, everyone forgot she would still by one of them and it would stop. Her wide curl could mesh with the circle of watchers at a touch and swing them into her motion.

It did stop. It stopped by Hecka. It held her shoulders, gripped her head, it put bars over her eyes, flat palms over her ears, a sealing finger over her mouth.

'Hecka.' said Lily.

'You cheated. You looked,' Hecka whispered, furious.

'Come on.'

The music played.

'I don't know anyone. I don't know everyone's name.'

'Don't worry.'

'I'm a worrier.'

'All right, worry. Come on.'

Hecka was led to the centre and blindfolded. The music came to an end. The blindfold was total. Hecka tried looking down her nose for points of light. There were none. She saw only the craze of changing specks in no colour. Reason said, in words: this darkness extends only an eighth of an inch from your eyes. Reason's enemy howled that the darkness was all there was, in her and beyond the same. I can't cope, she thought, knowing the rules doesn't help. She listened for a sound to re-establish the normal fixtures. A cough, tap, whisper would do. There was no sound. She felt herself begin to topple luridly twisted unsure what was up or down. Space had no markers. She remembered the childhood game when she had been lifted blindfolded higher and higher while the others chanted 'up . . . and up . . .' until her head banged the ceiling and it was not possible but true. When the blindfold was removed she had found it was illusion of credulity and fear: she had been lifted a mere foot from the floor and then a book tapped against the top of her head. Then it was possible but not true. Now she tapped the carpet with one foot to be sure of down.

'Lily,' she said, 'where am I?'

'In the middle.'

'I don't like it.'

Lily's voice was close to her ear. Where was she?

'It's where you always want to be. Now seek, Blind Man. Find us and you'll see again. Come.'

She turned Hecka by the shoulders, how many times round Hecka couldn't judge. The music began again, the same track.

> Where has your momma gone
> Where has your poppa gone

66

In my own way then, she thought. She lurched four clumsy steps this way, five another, how had Lily moved in such a small spiral? Hecka was afraid she would take twenty steps in a straight line and still not meet the circle because it would retreat as she advanced, or that she would take two steps and find herself far outside it, hearing voices and laughter moving further away in the darkness. Perhaps the way to know this place was to unwind it, to carry it with her by her own thread, but she did not dare.

Woke up this morning and my momma was gone . . . Her hands groped for contact. She set herself the tolerable fear of stumbling into a wheel chair and falling over. From outside she was making lumpish and pointless movements and did not even look funny.

'Careful,' a voice said.

She stopped and shuffled forwards. Her ankle met metal. She learned forward, stood wide for fear of falling and touched around. The arm of a wheelchair; a hand; an arm; a shoulder. Carefully, to touch the face. No face. No face. A round shape, wisps of hair, the back of the head facing the front? Was she outside the circle or in? The head lifted under her hands.

'Oh May, you've come, you've come.'

The party continued, willed it seemed to Hecka by Lily and by convention as inviolable as taboo; to say no to the one as difficult as to say yes to the other. Fat Edna was the only unpredictable element, a fret rubbing the predictable rite of the day. Orange squash and sweet sherries in small glasses were served by nurses to patients, with small sweet biscuits. Visitors got tired of talking, the nurses grouped themselves away from the patients, the patients elected silence and privacy. One woman elbowed her glass onto the floor and there was a rush of nurses with tissues to clear the small mess. Only two patients drank quickly and with pleasure; Edna drained her glass and heaved out of her chair, a moment of alarm, to fetch more liquor without being offered, and Mrs. Harris drank hers down and her face flushed pink and she went to sleep. Hecka refused sweet sherry, asked Lily where the whisky was, and took. It was a relief when the Friend of the Hospital played the Hokey-Cokey tune on the piano. A small circle formed without coercion. Hecka found she was drunk when she stood up. Edna glared and was the first to take up position.

> Your put your right arm in
> You put your right arm out
> You put your right arm in
> And you shake it all about . . .

Edna bellowed and her arm and fist punched into the circle. When she turned around thuds landed on her neighbours. She challenged anyone to disagree that that was what it's all about. She grabbed the wrists of the players nearest her for the rush into the middle.

> Oh Hokey Cokey Cokey

She was the first to the centre and the first out, warping the movement into a clumsy wave. Hecka, drunk and much taken with the bravado, tried to imitate. By the time she was putting her left leg in and her left leg out, she felt she could storm the centre with Fat Edna as her warrior queen. The waves grew chaotic, the singing louder. The move to the centre mattered. Lily had left the room to make tea. Hecka was trying to crash the circle, drag it with her into the middle, there were collisions and laughter. She was full of courage. When she put her whole self in, her whole self out and Cokeyed for the last time to the middle Edna got there first, the circle broke links, Hecka fell over and twisted her ankle, and Lily came and strapped it up.

*   *   *

'What's wrong with the patients in this ward?' Hecka asked Lily.

'All sorts of thing. You want tea?'

'Look around. You want milk?'

'Yes please. Have they had operations?'

'Some. That enough milk?'

'Yes ta. But they're so mixed.'

'Yes. That strong enough?'

'Yes. What kind of ward is it?'

'B Ward. Sugar?'

'No thanks. What's wrong with Fat Edna? And Mrs. Harris?'

'She's sick. And she's old. Biscuit?'

'No thanks. I mean, medically, why are these women all in the same ward?'

'The doctors decide. You really want answers or you just stuck on questions? Drink your tea it's getting cold.'

*   *   *

When Hecka got to B Ward to meet Lily at the end of a shift, she wasn't there. A nurse told her that Lily was being talked to by the sister. Knowing the difference between talking and being talked to, Hecka wondered what was up. It was the ward tea-time so she made an effort and sat on a spare chair at the end of a table where patients were drinking tea from blue plastic cups and picking at madeira cake. The woman next to her was talking.

'. . . Didn't you hear her in the night? You must've. I couldn't sleep a wink for her carrying on. There's no call for it, language like that . . .'

'What's she got anyway?' the other patient asked.

'I asked the nurse. What's she got to carry on like that for? I said. We're all sick people here, we don't carry on like that. She had an accident and they operated on her leg. She crashed her car or something. Shouting all night.'

What's she doing here anyway? There's a place for them in post-op.'

'She'd been in there and was getting on nicely so they gave her a chance here, more's the pity. I felt washed out this morning. Set me right back. Got some tablets from the nurse but they don't help.'

The other woman chorused, keep the comfort going.

'Due for another night of it, I suppose.'

She sighed the sigh of the long-suffering and picked the brown crust off her piece of cake.

'They moved her back early this morning. Some

complication. That's what she was carrying on about. All the same, no call for f---ing and blinding all night. Called the nurse a cow, I heard her. Keeping us all awake. As if we haven't all got troubles. Wouldn't be here else, it stands to reason. Got to make a show of themselves, some people. Don't seem to see how they show themselves up for what they are. A cow, she said: help me you cow. And calling out for drugs, more drugs all the time. She was already out of her mind with drugs. That's the only excuse I can find for her. I reckon that's when you get to know what someone's really like, when they're a bit pushed, got a bit of trouble or pain to cope with. That's when they show their true colours. Moaning and wailing, and called the nurse a cow when she touched her.'

She breathed righteously and drank a little tea as if it were a medicine, her mouth puckering as the taste afflicted her.

Hecka's proper sense of the proper line between herself and other people was broken again. She was being attacked but had no language and no right to intervene. Lily would crush these women: friends of hers would chip in with friendly argument. Both would change things a bit for the better. Hecka knew if she tried to speak for the injured woman, who might be suffering gross pain, she'd only harden the heart of the plump woman who was nursing herself and her injury so well. The two patients shared a peculiar intimacy, cradling their tea cups and their petulance, comfortable victims. Hecka wished she'd waited outside.

'Shouldn't be allowed. Got no shame. Keeping us all awake. You must've heard her?'

' . . . I had a bad night, tossing and turning. Woke up in a muck sweat this morning.'

'There you are then. Spoilt your sleep. No consideration. Shouting for drugs; help me you cow. I reckon she's an addict. Probably drugged when she was driving: brought it on herself. And who knows? There might be some little kiddy dead this moment from the likes of her driving in that state.'

She learned forward and clipped her cup onto the saucer, the final tap of the judge's gavel. The case rests there. Hecka's stomach for malice was tough, but she couldn't take it. Neither could she interfere without losing, she knew. She asked, to divert: 'Where's Mrs. Harris today?'

'Stuck in bed. She has her low days. Poor old soul. Better off dead at her age if you ask me. It would be a kindness.'

It soaked Hecka with rage. Puffy fingers crumbled cake and moistened it in the mouth with tea. Hecka drank hers down and went to wait for Lily in the corridor. A nurse passed.

'Excuse me, is Mrs. Harris all right?'

'Mrs. Harris? Oh yes. She gets a bit tired and stays in bed sometimes. She's all right. Do you want to see her? She's probably sleeping.'

'No, but if you have a moment, would you say May sends her love?'

'May? Yes, sure.'

Hecka waited. Lily came. Her face was flushed dark red under brown.

'Come on let's go from here.'

She got her coat and bag from the cupboard and they went.

'Who was the woman who was brought in from post-op?'

'I wasn't on. She'd had a crash. Smashed her hip and leg. Lucky if she walk again. Never able to bear children.'

'Was it her fault?'

'Hardly. She was in the passenger seat.'

'Why was she in B Ward?'

'She was doing well. But there was an infection and complications. Don't ask me; I'm only a nurse.' Lily sounded angry.

'What's the matter?'

'Come home with me and I tell you.'

As they walked, only three streets from the hospital, Hecka wanted to tell Lily about the woman at the tea table and hear Lily say the retort to them which would make it into a story, tolerable, which she could repeat to herself as if it really happened. Two things stopped her; one, a special kind of honesty, the disgrace of using fiction for reassurance and happy endings; and Lily's intense anger over something else, which required silence. As they reached Lily's house, the woman next door, at her dustbin, hurried inside and slammed the door hard.

'Huh,' said Lily.

Hecka had never been in Lily's place. It was a small front room with a mean bay, furnished by a landlord. Of Lily there was a Bible, a few clothes on a rail, and boxes of letters, bundles of letters, a table covered with them and with cheap notepaper and envelopes. Many letters lay open, and while Lily, still tight with rage, was putting a kettle on the miniature cooker, Hecka looked and saw they were all long and all to Dear Lily; Lily, Sister in the Love of our Saviour, Dearest Lily; Darling Lily. Several envelopes had foreign stamps.

'Lily, what's the matter, what happened?'

'You care?'

'I care.'

Lily took off her coat and uniform dress without reserve and put on a plain jumper and a print wrapper.

'You never see me angry before.'

'No. I knew you could be. It frightens me. Tell me.'

The kettle boiled and Lily made slap-dash tea, pouring hot water onto tea-bags in unwashed cups.

'Next door. She baby-minds. Piccanins she calls them. Talks to me sly and says 'they're so sweet when they're little'. Like none of us should grow up. I'm no piccanin and she knows it. I don't take notice, the world full of fools, she want trouble so I don't give. Then her husband standing at the gate talking with fat friends when he know I'm in here, saying we take all the jobs. I don't notice no rush of white girls wanting my job. Calling us dirty and he stink. She start to clean down her front step, all the paper and them, she never done before. Every day. She don't just clean down, she push all the dirt and rubbish to the door of this house. Every day. I get home tired, I sweep it away. Next day the same, and more because she put stuff there, beer bottles, potato peel, stuff that don't blow in from the street. Five days ago I go out and sweep it all back to her step. And then again. After three days her husband come while she watch from the door. She look really pleased like she got some big fighter, some big man, and she important woman so. He say I'm a pig, been troubling his wife. I say go away and ask your wife to speak truth. She call out "don't listen, they all dirty liars", but she don't open the door much. He threaten me that one dark night he catch me and show me what a white man do to trash. I pick up a milk bottle from the step and break it against the wall and tell him: you want blood to flow, it flow now, yours, and the dogs lick it up.'

'Lily . . .' said Hecka.

'What?'

'You frighten me.'

'I don't threaten you' . . . a twist of a grin . . . 'white woman . . . I threaten him. If you make threat you don't say sorry, excuse me, at the same time.'

'When did this happen?'

'Yesterday, after I get back from work tired and out of patience. I clear up messes all day and I come home and I get threaten if I don't clear up for the whole world all its messes.' Lily wasn't asking for sympathy. She was telling.

'You're still angry.'

'You think I should forgive, I'm a Christian, I don't feel? Let me tell you something: evil walk this world proud and raised up. If you want sympathy for the devil, go talk to his friends, not me.'

Hecka was told.

'Besides, he almost lose me my job today.'

'How?'

'They know where I work. He went up there and said I'd attacked him and his wife. Said they were in danger and I shouldn't be let near patients. Sister call me in just before you come. Perhaps she making sure I finish a duty before she suspend me. Don't waste nothing.'

'Didn't you explain what they'd done to you?'

'Yes. She say it make no difference. I should go to the police or take no notice, it's wrong to be angry if someone threaten you. She say: a Lady don't shout or break bottle. A nurse have position in society, got to be an example. I don't notice no position. I tell her I'm no lady. I defend myself all my life, no one else done it for me. So I should sit and smile and take no notice. The police come, sure, when there's what's left of me to cover with a blanket and carry away. That's what a lady do.'

'What about your job?'

'It's OK. They need me. They put a black mark on my folder so I don't get any fine idea about promotion. Didn't have none anyway.' Lily sniffed.

'What did the other nurses say?'

'They say they agree with me, but who know. People always say.'

'Lily, have you got a drink in the house?'

Lily opened a floor cupboard and brought out a half bottle of rum from amongst the scourers and disinfectant. They drank from the tea cups. Lily pulled the thin curtains and lit the gas fire. She sat in the one arm chair without any nonsense of offering it to Hecka. She needed it more. With the table lamp shining, the hiss and warmth of the gas fire, and the grey street shut out, the place became Lily's. She pushed off her shoes and drank.

'Do you want me to go?'

'No.'

'Do you feel safer now?' Hecka asked.

'Safe?' Lily gave the word back as if it were wrong currency.

'I mean: don't you need someone, a husband like she's got next door?'

Lily swigged.

'The man who marry me, he not born yet and his mother dead.'

The rum worked quickly. They were both tired and hungry. Hecka saw the scuffed slippers by the bed, the plain cross on the wall, and again the covering of impersonal surfaces with drifts of letters.

Hecka had met Lily at an evening class called 'Brush Up Your English', a title which later, with experience, she saw as dubious as 'Brush Up Your Morality' or 'Brush Up Your Life'. Lily came because she had to read and write specialised medical language, not a lot, but it was a nuisance at work. She was given Hecka to work with because she had a single need, and the tutor was free to work with the other students. At first Hecka found Lily dour. They worked apart from the others, but joined in when they wanted to. Lily took as many initiatives as Hecka. Hecka's respect grew. One evening the students were discussing poverty.

'Money don't matter,' a woman said.

Lily broke in. 'That's what the rich say. If you're poor, no one looks after you. The rich don't give to the poor. The poor give to the poor.'

And Hecka: 'And the poor give to the rich.'

They looked at each other and Hecka smiled. Lily's eyes narrowed. She made a 'huh' of acquiescence.

All these letters in her room: she must write a lot to get so many, Hecka thought, and knew she had indulged some patronage to Lily in the days of the English classes.

'Who are all these people who write to you?'

'Friends. I always write. One, two letters a day after work.'

'So many friends. And you keep their letters.'

'Every one I ever like. Back from school, some. People I work with. Don't you?'

'No, I only talk.'

'You miss a lot. If you write regular, little things, people do the same for you. The Book tell me the big thing, and letters tell me the small thing. I don't need no novels or make-up stories. Sometimes a friend write and tell me what she do or think and it all change. This place don't mean nothing.'

Her gesture wiped out the dipped bed, mottled carpet, flimsy curtains, walls and places beyond. The footsteps of other tenants passed right outside her door, creaking the floorboards inside her door. The cross hung bare on the wall. The next-door neighbour was very close. Thin curtains barely closed. The letters lay open and available. Lily poured some more and drank. The angry colour had gone from her face.

'This is not my country.'

'England?'

'Nowhere.'

'Your country is the world?'

'No. It's in here and in here.' She touched her breasts.

Hecka thought: she writes letters to friends and loves and never sees the letters again. She wished she could see some that Lily wrote. She gives them away, exchanges them, a story for a remembrance. She dedicates and writes and doesn't expect immortality, money or a name for herself. It was unlikely that all her friends kept her letters, or would put leather bindings around them.

'Have you ever thought of writing a book?'

'No. What for? Anyway, you know I make mistakes. You can't make mistakes in books.'

'Do you write to Mrs. Hibbert?'

'Yes. Once a week.'

'And she writes to you?'

'Yes, she tell me about the house, and Ed, and when I was young. Ed don't like it, so she send secret.'

'Subversion.'

'Whatever that mean. I don't know.'

'Truly. Sub-version.'

'Anyway, I've got all her letters. In that box.'

A big cardboard supermarket box was next to the bed, three quarters full of them. 'Did you get any letters this morning?'

'Yes, two. On the top there.'

Hecka was jealous of this wealth. She fetched two long letters from the table and read. Lily made slow toast at the gas fire. One letter was from Thailand. Lily explained the woman had worked with her and was a medical missionary now in a Thai village. The letter was full of chirrups of affection, requests for news of people Hecka didn't know, details of rain storms, village arguments, new patients at the field hospital, dry jokes about God's provision falling short in respect of certain medicines, and sweets which she craved, and an account in answer to a question from Lily of the arrival of a new and expensive cage-bird costing several hundred pounds, hanging outside its owner's house and uttering not a cheep, while all the other cage birds, a village passion, sang cheaply the whole day. Was it slippy trivia? It lacked grandeur. Hecka read it twice, absorbed.

The other letter came from the Midlands. Lily told her the woman had been a patient five years before, when she was having her third baby. The letter was broken and full of distress. The woman had tried to kill herself by eating twenty aspirin. That was all she had. She didn't even lose consciousness fully. When she was taken to hospital they pumped her stomach, abused her for not thinking of her children, and

76

mocked her for being silly to think that twenty aspirin would kill her. It was the mocking which hurt most. Never mind being too incompetent to live; she was incompetent to die.

'What will you say to her?' Hecka asked.

'I don't know.' Then: 'You ask question. D'you always think there's an answer?'

'I'm glad when there isn't', said Hecka.

They ate toast and Hecka went home.

She walked elated. She had been audience to the malice of the women at B ward tea-table, to Lily's rage and her telling of her neighbour's married complicity against her, and the ward sister's self-satisfied and blind judgement; she had been a looker-on at Lily's life of frugality and her rich expenditure of ferocity and love. At a remove she had handled the sheets of paper written by two remote women, one elegantly reporting a life which compassed, perhaps controlled, both God and little cage birds, the other near breaking and being mocked because she hadn't the competence to suffer in the proper style. Neither, it seemed, by the world's standards, did Lily, nor the woman in hospital with a broken body.

Petty, dependent, whining, vicious, stupid, incompetent; in part, in her heart, Hecka made all these judgments. Was that all? She had not wept, or stormed, or interceded. Lying in bed, the words 'help me, you cow' kept her awake for a long time.

*   *   *

4. The Rough Rite

It is an extremely painful and dangerous way to live
– split between a publicly acceptable persona, and a
part of yourself that you perceive as the essential,
the creative and powerful self, yet also as possibly
unacceptable, perhaps even monstrous.

Adrienne Rich

When Hecka was very young she was sense-linked as maybe all babies are. To her, sounds were colours were shapes were tastes. It was remarked on by adults because it appeared as abnormal statements. It should, in the normal process, have been wiped out in favour of distinct incompatible codes at the time when she was learning passively to understand language, but it hung on for a while. Fortunately she was not an indulged child and no one asked her to do party pieces of her peculiarity, as in 'I don't like the taste of the blue bells' (how quaint) so it never became an affectation.

Sooner or later she stopped saying silly things and didn't know that she chose colours because of their taste or how her skin received them. Even in her middle years though she was occasionally surprised, as when a chemical smell from a factory produced a shrill sound and a cone forming which she felt the shape of, not just with her hands. There was only an unusual, unpleasant smell, not comparable to any smell she knew. But there was also a noise and shape of a dull silver metal in the making and a dull taste in the mouth. The same thing happened three times. She kept quiet about it.

When she was young, but had language, she had a dream of paradise, a place which began with her wading through cold stream water which pushed against her steps and made her legs ache, over rough stones which hurt the soles of her feet. She was making her way across towards the far bank. The sharp stones and the force of the water made her unsteady, it was dangerous, but she would cross. At the far side was a mud bank rimmed with grass, so high she couldn't see the land above it. She grabbed and slipped at the brown mud, not knowing why she was set on seeing over the top. Mud, water and stones all fought against her. She clung and climbed until she could just see over the grass edge of the bank. What she saw was paradise.

She woke as her fingers slipped squeaking through the wet blades of grass and she slid back down the brown mud. It was enough. Paradise couldn't be described, so: there were colours, yellow, green, blue, like pictures in a Christmas annual and they were sounds. There was no familiar landscape. She woke, knowing that what she had seen was paradise conceptually, and as joy. The struggle and sensations to glimpse it were part of the vision. It would not have been what it was without the sharp stones, ache of water, the struggle to grip the mud and grass. They were paradise too. It was nothing to do with a tough pilgrim's progress through a vale of tears to a celestial city part I, blank page, and part II.

Perhaps it was a dying child's memory of the lovely world, of tumbling, climbing, grass, stones, wet and baked earth, vertigo, stingers, cold air, water, hotness, round, smooth, soft, scratchy, hard, mushy, edged, touching the world without opinions or the yip of statements.

Of course she got older and ordered and learned not to touch, but to use her head and contact the world with ideas and a limited range of textures, most of these by hand because the rest is shod and clothed. Muffled by clothes and constraints, the things she touched were mostly habitual, numbed. Inside her clothes, they became what she touched and enjoyed and suffered the feel of, wool scratch, leather press, the slip of jersey. She had preferences. The only way she pressed against the world, the other, apart from shocks of pain from which she normally enough ran for protection and padding, was when with the immediacy of children, by touch, she made love or, more rarely, struck out.

Then, as in the dream, there was no paved way to the far bank where colours are sounds and glorious, and no language adequate and without whimsy for the territory of her lover's body, for the stones, cold water, claw and slip of mud; the extremes are worded for pain or pleasure, to omit the word 'or' would drop her in the distinct word shit of the world's contempt; in abandoning the discrete she would lose discretion, in re-naming the proper version she would be named as pro-perversion.

But she had seen paradise, all the same.

*   *   *

Hecka looked at Aagot's small strong hands. The veins showed on the backs. She made no limp gestures with them. They were full of power and she knew it. Aagot chose to give them up to her by her will and then her wrists were so delicate Hecka could snap the small bones. They would not break.

Hecka did not know the difference between strength and weakness any more. They seemed to be the same and there was no word.

She did not know the difference between pain and pleasure. They seemed to meet here and be the same.

She did not know the difference between defeat and victory. There was no word.

She had suspected for long that these words were lies. Aagot made her face this impossibility.

Her cunt had its own will. It was a sea creature, an autist. It had no manners. It thought decided opened when it wished to receive closed firmly to rest and think and absorb slept and woke gave orders and submitted to them a queen a slave the perfect round animal blood black dark hot and endless, the maze, Hecka lost herself sightless and crying: only come, come, and I shall know the centre is wherever I am; your eyes are her messenger and I fear and adore them.

*   *   *

Hecka stood in the dole queue waiting to sign on for refusal of benefits. The thick plastic screens to protect the desk workers from the unemployed hardly seemed necessary. The queue for Box X15 was longest, snagging in loops, thickened where women had pushchairs and children. Someone remonstrated over the passing of two hours when she had somewhere to get to, but no one jumped the queue; something to do with no hope or at least low expectation of anything to be gained from fighting for precedence, softened the edges of contact. The thick man who would shove her out of the way anywhere else so that he could be in front said a soft sorry when he brushed against Hecka. A woman with a long and hopeless plea to make was given her time without any muttering from the people behind her. In a shop she would have been recriminated by the other customers. Here people waited like the hopeless, crouched for hours on a railway station, with no confidence that reaching their destination would be better than where they were. Perhaps they should storm the barricades: but to Hecka it felt fine. She needed it; the sedated sleepiness, a state just short of dream. Children ran and played and were looked at kindly.

On her first appointment she carried a book to blunt boredom, the edge of accidie. She didn't need it. From the first time, when she filled a form and got a bit of wooden bench to sit on, women talked to her about their lovers, children, landlords, death and hopes.

On later visits she stood in a queue with less talk but a lot to see. Eyes met and were sleepy. In the absence of contemplation, which she couldn't manage because she lost her temper when she tried, standing in a long queue there made her passive and gentle. And in that state things happened.

His eyes are too widely spaced and too wide open. One is hazel, one is grey. The white shows all round the iris. They are fixed on his mother's face, whatever she does, he sees only her, if he sees more it is part of her: because of the grey and hazel, it seems he sees twice, with difference. She grabs him up, his round belly pressed against her breasts.

'Give us a cuddle. Go on, give us a cuddle.'
His arm across her shoulder drops limp. She grabs it and puts it back.

'I said give us a cuddle.'
His arm slips slowly down her T-shirt and hangs limp. He watches her, smiling.

'Little bleeder.'
Her voice is affectionate. She slaps the side of his head. He holds his gaze and doesn't move at all from her slap. She slaps again three times.

'What did I tell you? What did I tell you to do?'
His smile and eyes widen. The last slap rings. People look. She leans to a woman friend sitting on the side of a pushchair and slaps the side of her head experimentally.

'Did that hurt?'
'Give over, will you.'
The friend looks away at a fixed point on the empty floor.

She takes his arm and bites it. Quickly he pushes a finger into her ear. Hecka can see it is a trick he learned from her.

'Ouch. Stop that. That bleeding hurts.'
He laughs and does it again, tangling his fingers in her hair as she pulls his hand away.

'Did you see him do that?'
Her friend withdraws and smokes and looks at the floor. The mother takes his arm and bites it again. He laughs with delight. She pokes his ribs with her fingers. Hecka winces. The boy doesn't move. She bites his face and his eyes don't flicker. She slips him down her body and hangs him upside down, holding his legs. He can't see her but his wide eyes are still full of her. She slips him as if she means to let him fall on his head. He screams with joy. Three times she shows him she can kill him if she chooses. She stands him on his feet and he goes limp.

'Fucking nuisance.'
She tugs him upright and he sags. She puts a hand on each side of his face, covering his ears, and begins to lift him from the ground so by his head.

'When I get you home you know what I'll do? I'll put you in the oven and roast you. Roast you alive.'
She turns to her friend.

'He believes me, y'know. He believes I will. He believes everything I say.'

Other people are observing sideways with disgust. Hecka is frightened. She knows the mother loves him, and he worships her.

*   *   *

Hecka phoned Aagot to suggest an outing for their planned evening together that day. It was an hour before they had arranged to meet.

'I can't make it,' Aagot said.
Hecka had not yet had time enough to know how much wiser it would be to say 'what a shame. See you soon then.'

'Why not?' she said. 'We arranged it. I've been looking forward to it all day.'

'It wasn't definite. I only said we could go out tonight.'

'I thought that meant we were going.'

'The Group is meeting.'

'But you don't usually meet on Thursdays.'

'Zina can't come on Friday. And we think it's important that everyone comes. It's a Priority.'

'And I'm not?' Hecka fumbled for a cigarette.

'We can go out another night.'

'Why didn't you phone and tell me before?'

'I've been busy.'

'It would only take you five minutes.'

'I would have phoned you later.'

'How much later? I'm getting ready to go out with you now.'

'We agreed in the Group that our meetings are a Priority.' Aagot sounded crisp, pressed. 'I must go now and tidy the place.'

'It's last night, isn't it,' Hecka said.

'I don't know what you mean.'

The burden of trying to say was too great with Aagot impatient, withdrawn, and wanting her off the line. A knife hung and you have to be in a fit state for surgery.

'Do you love me Aagot?'

There was a pause, which was a statement. Then: 'Yes.' It sounded as if she had weighed many things before answering and reached a moderate, balanced, all-things-considered conclusion. Hecka then was silent, hurt, but with no just base from which to cry: you have demoted me, if I am not first, then I have no place. Aagot knew there was trouble in the silence and did not want it dwelt on and developed.

'I'll ring you later tonight if I can. I have to go now.'

When the phone was put down Hecka realised too late that Aagot had not committed herself to phoning later, that she had not said when she intended to cancel their arrangement, when could it be since she was already getting ready for the Group? And that she had avoided talking of their last night together. Hecka was confused, degraded, and ignorant and felt that she was a fuss about nothing. It seemed she had been answered in all reason, but she felt fobbed off, punished. And she knew why.

She sat on her bed, weary, her bag by her side, dressed to

feel good to meet her lover, and tried to muster anger, a good resort in times of trouble. It was too dangerous. She knew she would sit there all evening waiting for the possible phone call, that if it came and she were angry she would lose Aagot. It was as simple as that. She knew her true condition. Under any arrogant talk, pride, and joy, she was dependent, a maiden aunt, the poor cousin who must earn her keep, her place at table, in bed, become a side-stepper, a diplomat, tip-toe away from doors shut in her face.

It was not bearable, not even possible. For the only time in her life the arrogant talk, pride and joy had been given rampageous freedom. She knew that freedom must not only be granted but taken for granted and she didn't have the courage to take, only to walk in where a door was open to her, not to shove and enter.

She fetched the liquor she had bought for the two of them to drink later that night and began drinking steadily, measuring, drawing spun threads from the thick confusion. The night before had been wonderful, full of wonders. Plainly it had not been so for Aagot and so should not have been for herself. She drank and remembered and was comforted by her room and its mess. The green light from the lamp was soft on the pictures, books, the bed where she lay now and where last night she had lain with Aagot and they had talked and beautiful things, she thought, had happened. She got up to look in the mirror and saw that she was still transformed from that time, her hair shone with silver, her body was fine. It became less and less likely that she had rightly understood the phone conversation with Aagot. Aagot could not be angry. She must have been sadly pressured by the Group to alter the meeting, and upset. She kept under the thought that Aagot might, at that moment, be presenting her, her talk and tentative actions, as problems to a group of women. Aagot would not betray her so. She loved her. The liquor hit. Nothing takes precedence over I love her so much she loves me. I am getting drunk and that's fine. She curled on the bed in her coat and the uninvited voice spoke unguarded. There was a whisper in her ear and it talked nonsense.

I was born once. You can hardly get away with less. Only

holy innocents go from warm darkness to the same, not knowing, back to the pulse they felt in us. We toll the tides with our aching effort, we pull the moon. It costs us blood. Only the sterile seed which falls on a stone is spared.

I was born once, as we have arranged it, mercifully, I knew no more of it ever again except what dead words dismiss of the cry of fear and cold ignored, ignored. I got on with things. I was just learning to get on with them quite well, on nodding terms, how to slither with unobtrusive charm, to slide-slip the foot which would crush me and to say sorry at the same time, to be busy, to form modest opinions. I was shaping up nicely into politics, a diary, a measured pace and reasons, and age.

And then I was born again. What earthly mother would be so cruel?

The whisper was small and strident.

Go back to your room, you are a bad girl, so bad you will stay there until I let you out again.

Why? Why?

Always stupid questions. Because I say so.

No, love, mother, no. I have bled enough to soak the world, I am coming to an end of bleeding.

What folly. I have the key. I am the door. I am your entry and exit.

Let me walk past. I cannot breathe; you take my breath away. I cannot speak; you web my lips with skin.

I will it.

Why?

Because I am impelled to. I am a maker, a mother, your love. It is what I am. I am here to open the doors and force you in, making your fingers which clutch at the doorposts. I will break them if I must. I am here to drag you out, crushing the bones of your head, if I must, as you fight for stillness and sleep. Do not ask me why. Do not be so stupid. I am here to do violence. You have given violent birth in your turn. Now it is mine. I wish you no harm. I am indifferent to it. I suffer it.

Be born with me then: be born with me and then we shall be saved, mother and child, lover, love.

No, that is not the way it is. That is too easy. Come willingly.

Do not seduce me with your loveliness, do not coerce me with your strength, my love, into a world where I will be hungry and you cannot feed me, do not open my mouth for kisses and leave my lips to crack and bleed dry, do not force me open, let me be, I can manage this, now.

I have no choice, I make life and it is pain. I do not choose, but if I did, I could, I would still so.

Be born with me then.

I cannot. My time will come and you will be unable to comfort me then.

But one opening is enough.

No, for you it seems not.

Could you not have run away from me, didn't you know?

I knew and did not know. If I had folded my body against the cascade of gold, the flood of stars, if I had walked away from you I would have circled to you again, it would not have been different.

I blame you, I curse you deeply.

So. I bear it.

I am too old. This time I cannot forget. There is no lapse, no drug to stun me. I cannot cobble a shabby cloth to wear again. You will button and bind me in saffron silk and pearls. I will grow beautiful, my hair will be thick and moving, I will be like a god, then you will look at me sightless as opal and I shall stand in my ridiculous raiment and my burning body alone, alone. Why do you do it? You cannot love me. You would not hurt me.

You fool. I am the awakener, the star of the morning, not the comforter. I am the maker of love, and pain, and all that which is not empty.

Leave me empty then.

No. I cannot. I shall fill you with scalding ikor and you will burn and melt and start again.

I do not want to be born again. Once is enough. I am too old.

It is not.

A circle of laughter, a ring of bright girls shouting
> See see see my mammy
> come out and play with me
> come out under the apple tree

kiss me kiss me
cuddle me cuddle me
tell me that you love me
you love me
tell me

They break hands and scatter to the crow of a metallic bell.

You don't know nothing, Hecka said startled, waking. At ten-thirty drunk, she woke fully and picked up the phone. An unknown woman's voice told her the Group was meeting and it was their collective decision not to receive calls in meeting time. It absolved Hecka from all anger with Aagot. It was not Aagot's fault. She was under discipline. By spreading the absolution thin it could cover all events, even those which had nothing to do with Group decision. Hecka took off her coat and slept well.

*   *   *

DRAMATIS PERSONAE

ZINA   )
AAGOT   )
FAY   ) women, members of the group
MAY   )
STELL   )

SCENE

The kitchen of AAGOT's house on a winter's evening. Centre, a table with wooden chairs, above, a poster on the wall. Stage right, a sofa with cushions. Usual kitchen fixtures.

AAGOT, FAY and MAY are seated at the table. ZINA sits cross-legged on the sofa. Curtain rises on laughter and vague conversation ('I'm not sure ... perhaps it would be a good idea ... I can't see anything against it ...') A short pause.

AAGOT: Do you have phantasies?
           (laughter)
MAY: Sure, I have one every morning. That today will
           be OK.
AAGOT: Sexual phantasies, I mean.
           (laughter)

90

ZINA:	I used to. I needed them when I was in relationships with men. I don't need them now.
MAY:	Yes, but a lot of women do though.
AAGOT:	Why do you think that is?
	(she gets up to make coffee, stage back)
ZINA:	Well, when you think what a bad trip sex is for most women, it's not surprising if they find something better in their heads. There's a lot of research going on in America. On the East Coast mainly.
AAGOT:	What kind of research?
ZINA:	Well, general, you know. And some of the women who have problems are getting together to explore them in interaction.
AAGOT:	What, do things, you mean?
ZINA:	Yes, with agreement about the limits, and safeguards built in. Some of them are getting near the sources of their internalised oppression and finding they are freed from it. It's like the tyranny of orgasm.
MAY:	And then what are they left with?
ZINA:	What do you mean?
MAY:	When they don't have phantasies and don't have orgasms. What are they left with?
ZINA:	I would have thought that is the whole point. They aren't 'left with' anything. They are free to discover themselves without distortion by the demands of capitalist sexuality.
MAY:	Well then, what are they discovering?
	(AAGOT *hands round coffee.*)
ZINA:	You can't disengage yourself from oppression and make a new life just like that. They are finding what they really want and need, how to nurture themselves. But of course there's backsliding into old ways.
	AAGOT *takes the ashtray from the table, empties it into a bin, wipes it, puts it back on the table*
MAY:	Backsliding?
ZINA:	Yes. Some women don't have their consciousness

raised enough to cope with what's going on. They slip back into the old habits of phantasising about dominant men. They resort to orgasm that way because it's something they get false security from. When they're not faking it, of course. Look, could we speak about something else? It seems to me that this is self-indulgent.

MAY:　　　＼
AAGOT:　 ） Why? Who's being self-indulgent?

ZINA:　　　We live in a world where women are raped, economically exploited. Why waste our time talking about all this rubbish in women's heads? It will go when sexism dies.

(silence)

AAGOT:　　I wanted to talk about it.

FAY:　　　I wanted you to talk about it, too.

ZINA:　　　Give me one, good, reason why.

AAGOT:　　There are two good reasons why. Fay and I want to talk about it.

ZINA:　　　It seems clear to me, if one is to get anywhere in a group discussion, that its content must be evaluated.

MAY:　　　I don't come here to be evaluated.

ZINA:　　　I mean what we talk about. You know perfectly well what I mean.

MAY:　　　Yes, I think I do.

(silence)

FAY:　　　What's a phantasy?

(laughter)

FAY:　　　I thought I knew, but now I'm not sure.

ZINA:　　　Phantasies are dreams, ways of pretending that everything is all right. When what's really happening isn't all right at all ... Well, aren't they? ... What else? ...

AAGOT:　　I don't know, but aren't phantasies part of what's really happening? And a lot of phantasies women have are about submission, cruelty and pain even. How can that be pretending everything is

92

	all right? I don't see how it can give pleasure, but it does.
ZINA:	Distortion. Colonisation of the mind. Mindfucking.
MAY:	(to AAGOT) Why did you want to talk about it?
AAGOT:	I didn't.
MAY:	But you said . . .
AAGOT:	I only asked if you had phantasies.
MAY:	Why?
AAGOT:	I thought it would be interesting to talk about.
MAY:	It would be, yes it would be.

(Ring at the door. AAGOT answers it and STELL enters. The phone rings and ZINA goes to answer it. THE GROUP has agreed that phone calls in meeting time will be handled by someone other than the woman living there: it saves pointless tensions.)

CURTAIN

*   *   *

Aagot brought the problem of her lover to the group, because she thought that was a fair use of her woman friends and no harm to Hecka as long as she did not know about it. But she was astute enough to deflect the problem from herself and avoid being explicit.

They met in the kitchen for the warmth of the oven. Fay and May sat on wooden chairs at the table; Aagot out of habit occupying the chair at the head. It was her house. Zina took the displaced spare divan. Aagot had cleared the table and washed up. The women preferred to talk in kitchens; the exception was Zina's house, a 'non-sexist' mixed commune in which she was the only lesbian. There the group found their talk was colonised by slight bearded men who slipped in and sat uncomfortably, modestly, on boxes or the floor and listened to the women talking. Their silence was impeccably unobtrusive and intruded grossly.

The ancient obsequies took over and the women found themselves speaking in a manner which waited on answer from the men. The pauses between words, spaces full of substance for the women, were perceived by the men as empty places for them to occupy. On their model, if nothing was heard to be happening, nothing was. Vacant lots were for development. The women let them do it and listened with gruesome tolerance to what they said. Any talk about male behaviour was defused by the men with persistent liberal reason. When Stell had begun to ask 'Why do men vandalise . . .' she got no further; the men present hastened to dissociate themselves from such charges and to suggest that since they were representative, and innocent, there was nothing more to be said. Stell persisted, owl-eyed with irritation.

The defences became absurd. Men are oppressed at work, at school (far more than women and must give it expression) if a few men piss in phone boxes it is because they are caught short, a peculiarly male problem, and out of decency seek the privacy of a brightly lit phone box rather than offend women by exposing themselves at the curb: well yes, men and boys do shit in tower block lifts, but that's so that they won't disturb the family they care so much about by pulling the lavatory chain when they get home late at night: and so on, and so on. The exclusively scatological nature of vandalism was the men's choice of emphasis. It excluded violence and defined the acts as pursuit of natural relief. Stell felt she had fallen into a bog. Fay, May and Aagot didn't support her. They listened. Zina gave weight to the men's words by debating with them, debate was her joy, but afterwards the other women revolted. May said they were walking into a trap, an old trap: it was hopeless to walk in and try to smash it from inside. Better to walk away and leave it empty. Leave the men to wonder why the old baits didn't entice. Zina disliked this tone and argued the need for the women to stay; it was not a trap but neutral ground and women must occupy it, become the peers of men in discussion, help the men to understand. She did not feel trapped. It was women's responsibility to enter into dialogue. How else was the world to change? Aagot said she didn't know how the world was to change, but she knew she felt ill at ease and wondered what the men were getting out of it. The women were unable that time to act on their objections.

The change came one evening when the women were talking about Rape Crisis Centres at Zina's house. Two men drifted in in a non-sexist way, and spoke about violence done to men by women in the home and about children battered by their mothers. While they were speaking another man was chopping wood salvaged from a derelict house, to use for the fire, just outside the kitchen door. It was difficult to object to. He was doing a domestic and caring job with conservational overtones. The crash and splinter frightened Stell, Aagot and May. The axe seemed to be directed at them, a gross physical threat backing the men's demand that the women admit to being the original sources of blood and pain. The threat of the axe was frightening. Zina felt it, but as another responsibility to shoulder. Fay absorbed it as she did all pain, without knowing she was injured. She menstruated heavily two weeks out of four and was weak with anaemia. She was, as such are seen, the most attractive woman in the group; white and thin. The doctor gave her iron tablets in a form which her body could not absorb, and told her to eat nourishing foods. She ate but could take no goodness. Fay was dangerously weak. The doctor also advised her archly that things would improve if she led an active sex life. One reason she started coming to the group was to find out how you set about becoming a woman.

On the night of the axe her blood flowed fast and painfully. Her voice poured in a violent red flow, and ached with the constriction of padded silence. She said nothing. No one recognised that there was blood in the room.

The group insisted on meeting in Zina's chill bedroom. The men wraithed away when the women didn't offer to bring them into existence. Fay, Aagot, May and Stell felt better.

The wooden chairs in Aagot's kitchen are uncomfortable. They are hers and she doesn't notice any more. On the wall over the table a poster in puce pink and black asserts sisterhood is blooming. May thinks OK, OK, I submit. It reminds her of the writing on the pediment of the northern college she went to: something about culture being good for you, get it down you. It's not a joke she could share.

Aagot has been moving furniture all day, re-arranging her house as she loved to do. She feels relief in her shoulders as she lets go this final burden. She drops it cold and hard in the middle of the floor.

'Do you have phantasies?'

The thud is muffled with laughter from all four women. They have been talking about the politics of marching with a Gay Liberation Front demonstration. It is funny, such a non sequitur. And it needs barge-poles of mirth to stop the lump rolling to rest at the feet of any one woman. So it lies still, but bang in the middle of the room, unstable and indecent. Aagot drops it for someone else to pick up or poke at; she can admit possession, or maybe can't, perhaps chooses not to, but certainly doesn't. If anyone were to say 'Why do you ask?' she would reply 'I'm just interested.'

In this company she is wise. Hecka often stormed her, fascinated and raging, when Aagot performed such acts of power, tiny as adjusting the position of someone else's tea cup, massive as an oblique censure in making love. Aagot would simply say 'I only moved a tea cup: I only moved away. It means nothing.'

'Do you have phantasies?'

Aagot is secure in asking, because she doesn't, and can save that up to say at the best time if she needs to clear herself. She is stirred with pleasure and troubled by Hecka's dreaming, but knows that the group does not ask searching questions.

Last week they had discussed Orgasms. There was no plan to make it personal, but May had upset the dispassionate discussion of the prevalence of orgasm amongst heterosexual women by saying that she did have them. Zina objected to this breach in the code of debate and Stell, who hasn't come to this week's meeting and for whose absence May feels she is blamed, had found May's smiling statement oppressive to other women. May said she didn't want to oppress anyone, it was just that there was a long time when she didn't have them and now she was glad she did. Judgement was rife, but the breach of etiquette caused a brief blaze as such breaches do, bright enough to reveal that Fay didn't know what an orgasm was, Zina and Stell had orgasm by their own touch only, Aagot had climaxed with her husband but not with women lovers since. As the flare died Aagot was near to asking Fay why she had joined a lesbian group, as Fay had been wishing to be asked and helped to the answer for some time: but as Zina said, all this was hardly helping move the discussion forward, and commonsense prevailed.

May wants to keep quiet about phantasies on this night, so she makes a diversionary clatter.

'Sure. I have one every morning. That today will be all right.'

Last week she had defended herself as best she could, but had lost rating. She felt bruised, so did the others, but no one wanted to examine the injuries. This time she keeps quiet by banter because she is brave, but not stupid.

'Sexual phantasies, I mean,' says persistent Aagot.

Zina breaks the barrier of mirth as she often does, with seriousness and a desire not to waste time. 'I used to. I had them when I was in relationship with men. I don't need them now.'

There is a collective movement, crossing of legs, shifting back. It looks like relaxation, but no one feels it as pleasant. It is difficult to know what has happened. Silence is probably safest. The chairs creak.

Innocently, at least with no desire to do harm, Zina has blocked the way for any other woman who differs. She makes sure by her leadership that the group is safe: gives one pull on the lever and ensures that anyone who wants a different journey must resort to shunting about in the sidings while the others climb aboard once again for a grand tour of other women, their problems out there, oppressions and mistakes out there. It is a journey none of them wants to make again, but they all fear what seems to be the only alternative, jumping the rails, collisions, the threat of contact with the ugly obstacle Aagot has dropped.

May says 'Yes,' to Zina. She means no, not quite, and repeats 'Yes, but a lot of women do though.'

Aagot, who really wants this to be talked about, is relieved that Zina's signal has been challenged. 'A lot of women' can be as inclusive as you make it. Aagot says 'Why do you think that is?' and gets up to make the coffee. She is hostess for this week and can safely turn her back on the lump now that May is taking care of it. Aagot has made a contribution by asking the question. Now she is making the coffee. It would be unfair to ask more of her.

Here the track forks: the main line rackets on, maybe coming full circle, but it is the journey. The branch line goes nowhere but gives a respite from the company and the decision; you can sit alone and do some urgent knitting. Her few steps to the kettle and the cups are an ancient track taken by women to put themselves out of harm's way. When they return, as they have to, they find their place taken and their destination changed.

Zina is secure. Phantasy is an aspect of the oppression of women she can talk about from reading. No one has dared press her on her introductory 'I used to', or asked Aagot why she asked the question, or asked May which lot of women do though. It would be like asking Fay why she came to the group at all. The code is: that giving of secondary source information, each item placed like a playing card to lean carefully against another, will mount into a fragile tower. The placements are limited in nature. A shaking or violent hand or a breath of distress can collapse the whole game. The structure is ordained, there is no possibility of baroque or experimental, only a pleasant pagoda. Under the toy tower, a point in space, the toy train runs in its circle. Velocity and location appear at the moment of their meeting to be one. The old impossibility seems to be happening. We are getting somewhere. It is a lie.

They all experience the lie as distress. For Zina it is an ugly feeling that in spite of her efforts people and things are not shifting as they must to get somewhere and she blames. No one recognises the force of her initiatives, the strength of her mind and body.

For Fay it is fear, that something is happening but she is not there to perceive it. On some evenings she wanted to speak. She imagined her mouth opening and shapes of silence coming out, or a high sound like birds while the women would look with horror, and she would know that her fear was true and that she imagined herself. Alone in her room she would sit like a child with a pencil and scraps of paper writing her name

FAY

FAY

FAY PRICE...

Unlike most children she never extended it to Fay Price, London, England, Europe, The World, The Universe. She believed in the World but her name did not belong with it. She occupied no space. She occupied very little. Her chest was still, she hardly took her piece of air. Her movements followed those of the other women. If one moved her leg or put a hand to her face, Fay would try it too. She didn't feel contact with surfaces. She accommodated to the greater reality of wood or stone, and accepted the reality of a playing card tower.

For May, the lie of Getting Somewhere was a head-ache which hurt her every week and she wonders, as she does every week, why she comes. She is beginning to suspect a secret she couldn't say without being judged destructive and silly: that they are all playing with broken tools and toys, useless detritus; the tin track and the fingered cards have to go into the rubbish bin. Since she has nothing to offer instead, and thinks that Zina, Fay, Aagot and Stell are happy with the game, and she is happy for other reasons to be with them, she doesn't bother. On this Thursday night on Halt Hill she wants to stay. She likes Aagot's question. She feels affectionate and hopeful. Also, she fancies Aagot, which is dangerous. All good reasons for staying. She has always been an indolent mover.

There seems to be no chance of her doing anything about Aagot. A woman called June had belonged to the group for two months and in that indecently short time, in which surely a significant relationship could not grow, had made her feeling for Fay clear. Fay was overwhelmed, first by confusion and delight, then by the group which with Zina's direction made plain that pairing was disruptive to the open interaction of its members. Aagot felt this was harsh but maybe necessary, and acceded. May thought it was cruel and an avoidance of the heart of the matter, their being together as lovers of women which she had never understood to be a simple political passion. She was no mistress of debate and lost, without her accession being required. June was not present on the evening this was decided.

Fay did not know if she had been given a gift or had one taken away from her. Both June's offering, and the group's censure, were lovely and bewildering. Zina phoned June, finish.

'Yes, (no) but a lot of women do though.'

'Why do you think that is?'

Zina has an answer. 'Well, when you think what a bad trip sex is for most women, it's not surprising if they find something better in their heads.'

Phantasy then is what straight women do in their desolation. They, Them, Other; these are her words, conventional ways of uncovering conventional truths. She has saved many meetings of women from the pain of possible discovery by using them. She gets things done and is respected. Most Women means Other Women to Zina. Aagot suspects she is in this category. May knows she is. For Fay the question doesn't arise.

Zina's eyes look lucidly into faces when she speaks, but away from faces when they speak. She believes love is an historical fraud. To be alone is bad, to be with one other woman too enfolded, a-political. She lives communally and falls asleep as soon as she is on her mattress alone. Every evening she goes out to an event, social or political, except for the night she stays at home for a house meeting. Several women have lived in the house and left, but Zina will stay. She castigates those who do not have the commitment to come to every meeting.

Aagot, making the coffee, thinks: Zina is a bully. She reminds me of Hecka. Zina says 'There's a lot of research going on in America. On the East Coast mainly.'

The first tier of the pagoda is complete. The women have displaced themselves into other women. Now phantasy is in another land. Now it is in the hands of researchers.

Aagot is unscrewing the coffee jar. She asks 'What kind of research?'

She looks carefully at a spoon of coffee powder, considers tapping a few grains back into the jar, lines the cups in a row. Zina says 'Well, general, you know. And some of the women who have problems are getting together to explore them in interaction.'

It will soon be too late to cry havoc. Aagot's spoon goes scoop, tap, tap, scoop, tap, tap... 'What, do things, do you mean?' May is delighted with Aagot for the simple question.

'Yes, with agreement about the limits, and safeguards built in. Some of them are getting near to the sources of their internalised oppression and finding they are freed from it. It's like the tyranny of orgasm.'

May is hot and angry. She blushes. She thinks: I am not a tyrant. I am ferocious and soft. 'And then what are they left with?' she asks, and on the instant thinks hell, I'm doing it again.

'What do you mean?'

'When they don't have phantasies and don't have orgasms. What are they left with?'

Zina looks at May and recognises that she is talking about love, about Zina, about May. She has learned how to side-step such traps. She has been taught to transcend by masters. She does not need the support of others, it seems, and does not withdraw from a fight.

Zina wears layer upon layer of textured, brocaded, knitted fabrics; bronze ribbed stockings, sandals of criss-crossed woven strips, thick clothes in colours of leaves and bark. Her hair is a dense dull gold of small waves, her skin opaque. She is impermeable. Her presence is bigger than she really is. Some women feel a kind of gravity pull to her, that they could be drawn in, smothered. They breathe warm dust and fear. She usually sits with empty space around her, often, as tonight, displaced, on a different level from the other women, on the chenille covered divan among the patterned cushions.

May looks from Fay's face to Aagot. She hopes to find

some kindness, she needs support, but they are both occupied, Aagot pouring milk into cups with care that no drops fall, Fay tapping ash from her cigarette as Zina had just done.

As May looks again at Fay, her sight lurches, and she sees Fay's white face slowly turn the eye's original image: not reason, the mind's shift, until her eyes unmoving are changed by vertigo into a dead stare, her neck exposed, her face tallow and dead blue, a streak at the corner of her mouth which could be black blood from a lip torn with terror: a heat a dark stench of rotting fabric a laugh so high it could be a scream: there, then gone, impossible, common sight shuttering. Fay wipes a smear of coffee skin from the corner of her mouth. Zina is saying 'I would have thought that that is the whole point. They are not "left with" anything. They are free to discover themselves without distortion by the demands of capitalist sexuality.'

May has forgotten her vision because it is impossible. But she does not look directly at Fay again for the rest of the evening, and feels an unaccountable irresponsibility, a different context for herself, the others, this room and this time.

'Well then, what are they discovering?' She is smiling. She raises a heavy arm to take her coffee from Aagot and neglects to say the usual thanks. She is asking Zina what she knows of love, what she can name for herself. Zina takes her coffee without noticing. She knows what she has been asked. To her it is a battle of will. 'You can't disengage yourself from oppression and make a new life just like that. They are finding what they really want and need, how to nurture themselves. But of course there is backsliding into the old ways.'

Aagot thinks a purposeful discussion of facts is going on, but all the same she is irritated by Zina's voice. She has no words for her annoyance and no reason to cross the few feet of floor and demonstrate it. She takes the ash tray next to May from the table, stands up, walks to the waste-bin, empties the ash tray, wipes it, puts it back closer to May than it was before. May sips her coffee. She knows she has been named by Zina a back-slider, unenlightened. Aagot is tidying her up. Too much has happened and May is too indolent to care.

What is left of what she saw is this rich indolence. Aagot and Zina see it in her as a sloppy ease, almost a sneer, May at her most tiresome.

'Back-sliding?' May says smiling.

'Yes, some women don't have their consciousness raised enough to cope with what is going on. They slip back into the old habits of phantasising about dominant men. And they resort to orgasm that way because it's something they get false security from. When they're not faking it, of course.'

May hears: ... some women ... don't ... enough to cope ... slip back ... old habits ... false security ... faking. Zina is still speaking. 'Look, could we talk about something else? It seems to me that this is self-indulgent.'

Interruption is very rare in the group, but May and Aagot are compelled to speak.

'Why ... Why? ... Who's being self-indulgent?'

Zina talks on through them, a bit louder and clearer. '... We live in a world where women are raped, economically exploited. Why waste our time talking about all this rubbish in women's heads. It will go when sexism dies.'

For the first time in all their meetings Zina is aware of the silence then, and the physical space between her and the other women. It's not comfortable. She believes in what she has said but doesn't know why it has this effect. The silence lasts a moment too long.

Aagot says 'I wanted to talk about it.'

At last, Fay, 'I wanted you to talk about it too.'

May doesn't look at her. No one will help Zina. She has to go on fighting although she will not win what she wants now. She chooses Fay and looks at her, because Fay seems weaker than Aagot.

'Give me one, good, reason why.'

Fay is lost. Aagot answers from annoyance. 'There are two good reasons why. Fay and I want to talk about it.'

So, if will is the issue, Zina can win something. It is irresistible. 'It seems clear to me, if one is to get anywhere in a group discussion, that its content must be evaluated.'

Clear and reasonable; but May answers 'I didn't come here to be evaluated.'

Zina is exasperated. Surely to god May can't think that, can't misunderstand so deviously: of course she's not evaluating anyone, only the pertinence of the topic. 'I mean, what we talk about. You know perfectly well what I mean.'

'Yes,' says May, 'I think I do.'

Aagot understands both Zina's reason and May's unreason. She is immobilised. The silence empties them out. There is no way Zina, Aagot or May can move without collisions or danger.

Aagot is remembering her school essays, how she hated being evaluated as a B− or a C+, how she longed to be a straight A. How she hated to be graded at all and how she longed to be graded well. She thinks about Hecka's ravings about the need for judgment and herself saying no over and over again. She is reminded that it was a question from her about Hecka which started all this. Hecka's talent for disruption works even when she's not there. Mustn't let her into the group again.

Aagot looks up and catches May smiling at her. She smiles. Fay catches the tide and asks Aagot 'What's a phantasy?'

They all laugh with relief. 'I thought I knew, but now I'm not sure,' Fay says.

Is this what she is, that she can make her friends laugh? Is this her self, she made them laugh? They laugh and look at her, she can smile to them, is this who she is? When she was a baby girl she heard her mother talking to her father about her, and knew they were not pleased with her, and she was silent listening with joy although she was too little to understand what they were saying, and the joy was that they were gods who recognised her existence by speaking of her at all, and they could have chosen to kill her and she would have felt the joy of being chosen by the gods to be killed. Now she picks up attributions of clown cleverness, of stupidity, it doesn't matter. She floats in the warm fluid of her friends' laughter. Fay Price.

Out of habit Zina picks up the question. 'Phantasies are dreams. Ways of pretending that everything is all right. When what's really happening isn't all right at all . . . Well, aren't they? . . . What else?'

May is grinning hugely at Aagot. Aagot keeps her eyes on May while she answers, although it is Zina she is answering. 'I don't know, but . . . aren't phantasies part of what's really happening? And . . . a lot of phantasies women have are about submission . . . cruelty and pain even . . . how can that be pretending everything is all right? . . . I don't see how it can give pleasure, but it does.'

May is enchanted. Aagot has moved her arm a fraction of an inch, a long way, towards her while she was speaking. Some ash falls from May's cigarette onto the table and Aagot doesn't even notice.

Zina still has some awareness of the apparent content of language. 'Distortion,' she says, 'Colonisation of the mind. Mind fucking.' But she is lost. Her kind of lucidity leaves her alone. The silence belongs to Fay and May and Aagot. She feels the terror of being excluded from a group. It underlies her tenacity for control, this fear that if she isn't tenacious and useful she will be left alone, not included when friends are meeting, no phone call or post card. It has happened to her once or twice and left her in pain. Once she had arrived at a house for a meeting when the expected reminder hadn't come, to find everything going on without her and the others dismayed by her arrival. She was appalled, but stuck it out. It was one of her worst memories.

May wants Aagot to speak again so that she can watch her mouth. She asks her 'Why did you want to talk about it?'

'I didn't.'

'But you said . . .'

'I only asked if you had phantasies.'

'Why?'

'I thought it would be interesting to talk about.'

'It would be. Yes, it would be.'

Stell rings at the door. Aagot lets her in. The phone rings and Zina answers. Aagot doesn't hear the conversation, she is out of the room. When she returns Zina does not mention it. They talk of other things. The evening is lost, or gained.

At this rate we shall soon be absolved, or dead.

*   *   *

'. . . and all in all I'm a heavy weight slate-grey hanging rock of a bore; one kick of your decisive little foot and I'd be off my top spot thud on the ground, a stone among stones . . .'

'. . . What's that ugly great stone doing in the middle of your floor, Aagot?'

'That? That's my old friend Hecka.'

'The one who . . . ?'

'Yes.'

'But I thought she was . . .'

'No.'

'Can I stand my coffee cup on her? Is it safe?'

'Yes, do, she likes to be useful now.'

*

Zina is working with force and will. She is effective so, politically. She goes home and composes an astute letter which will oblige a councillor, in terms of his own political morality, to support the demands of a housing collective. So she is effective, does something for good which not every woman could do. Certainly no one else in the group could do it. They don't have the force, or the will.

In eighteen months Zina will begin a slow change, in retrospect a crisis. Its premonition is her fright this evening when she is aware of silences after her words. She leaves the group, blaming the women, but the silences and the fear go with her. She increases her activity but her solitude grows. She begins to stutter which is horrifying to her, the breakdown of speech. Language as a surgeon's knife is her weapon. She dreams of talking to men and she stutters, an ugly gaping of her throat on vowel sounds only, which jams open the outlet of breath and words and exposes her because she can't reach the end of a statement. She is vulnerable, her way out becomes their way in. She wakes from such dreams with shock as from a nightmare.

She is lucky. She meets a woman who wants her very much and who is tough. This woman can happily go on thinking in Zina's presence, is not available to be wiped out by her; a fierce and generous lover who loves her for her decisiveness and beauty, and at the same time is not conned by them at all.

106

Zina is lucky because she might never have met a lover big enough to take her and appreciate her. Most women do not.

Women are possessed by love, mastered, fondled, and dwindled. Survival and escape stories are the women's genre of our time. Women are elected for qualities they are bewildered to be told they possess; warm, sympathetic, gentle, understanding. If being so will reward them with embrace in burning wings and being carried up, up . . . in the end they are dropped. They are unfit companions for a flight which darkens the sky. They belong feet on the ground. They would be better armed with arrows and slings to bring down the hawks which darken their skies.

So Zina is lucky. She finds a companion, a grounded angel, an angelic groundling, like herself, to soften her delusions and also do her complex justice.

*   *   *

Some stories come out of this maker impossible to tell: they catch and vomit.
Fay Price.
She meets a man:
He is obsessed with her.
He begins to give her a name of his making:
He tells her what drinks she drinks, what films she favours, what clothes suit her.
He never calls her her name.
It begins to seem she is really here.
He takes her to bed and by his passion convinces her further.
She leaves the group because he does not like it:
So she does not like it.
When he is near she trembles:
He is excited.
She demands nothing:
Her white body and her blood excite him.
There is no limit to his power:
He beats her and slaps her and leaves bruises on her body.
Her cries of fear and tears excite him to greater passion:
She feels his joy and so it becomes hers.

She is terrified and entranced:
She does not discover as she might even so and also have
    done, the pleasure of pleasure:
Only the pleasure of pain.
He abuses and humiliates her:
She is proud and grossly humiliated.
Some of his physical actions are dangerous.
She tries to tell a woman friend what is happening:
The woman is embarrassed and prevents talk.
One night he splits her mouth and threatens her with death:
He thrusts her out of the flat in the late evening, keeping her
    coat so she will have to travel home in the slight dress he
    chose for her.
It is a cold night.
She catches a Circle Line train:
The compartment is empty.
Two young men get in:
They watch her.
They are excited by the thin shoulder straps of her dress, the
    high heels:
Above all by the smear of dark blood at the corner of her
    mouth.
The train is stopped by signals between stations:
They attack her.
She thinks of her lover's threat of death:
He is the whole world and these two men are part of the world
    he has made for her.
She expects to be killed:
It is no surprise.
This is the appointed night.
She knows now there is a relation between herself and the
    world:
For sure she is here.
At this point there is a life to struggle for.
The men run from the train at the next stop:
Her body falls and dies in a move towards the platform.
The doors jar as they close across her throat:
The guard tries again.
All trains are suspended on the Circle Line for half an hour:

Service is then resumed as normal.

*   *   *

Dole office in season again: stand and doze, blur and wait. A woman sits on the bench for First Time Signers with her baby daughter. The child is urgently unhappy. It takes Hecka a few moments to see the scale of misery; the child such a small being, the word fractious stands between. She screams and plucks her clothes, undoing the buttons of her white cardigan by pulling at the welt, a small garment rent, a small passion. The mother pushes her hand out of the way, not flesh against flesh, but a piece of machinery out of alignment, and does the buttons up again. When the crying gets louder the mother picks her up, an object of disturbance, and leaves her in the pushchair by the door. The girl cries more and is sick. The mother goes to the pushchair, takes the child out and puts her to one side, mops the chair clean with tissues, then wipes the cardigan and dress. Last and least she wipes the child's face with the dirty tissue and sets her on the floor at her feet. She does not speak. It is not usual to speak to things, even if they malfunction or are out of alignment.

The mother's name is called and she goes to the barrier. The baby is left sitting on the floor looking for her mother. She is desperate; her mother is out of her sights, she is too young to go search and has no belief that her mother still exists, she could be gone for ever. Her cries are not answered. She quietens for a moment lapsing into grief, and looks at the strange faces but does not recognise them as faces. There is only one she would know and it has left her.

Everyone around is variously troubled, some more angry, some fearful. It seems that no one can do anything. Three seats away an older woman leans forward while the child is quiet.

'Come,' she says, 'Come,' and gestures with her hands. She does not smile. Her voice is soft. The little girl screams again, this time directing her cries at the woman. When she grows tired and hushes the woman speaks, the same words and invitation. People around think maybe she is making it all worse, upsetting the child more, and worse still, beginning something which will result in the mother returning angry at interference.

'Come . . . come . . .' She does not get up or move towards the baby. 'Yes . . . come . . .'

The little girl bumps and crawls towards the older woman, the woman bends to pick her up carefully, all her movements gentle and slow not to scare her. She sits her on her lap, a hand holding her belly. She speaks in a whisper to her and wipes the tears from her face with her hand. She does not straighten her dress and cardigan or bother with the shoe the girl has left on the floor. She wipes her face with her fingers and talks to her.

When the mother has finished at the barrier and turns back to collect her child, Hecka turns away. She does not want to see. She knows anyway when the child has been put back in the pushchair, strapped down against movement, fixed. She knows by the outcries of indignation and refusal to be dead.

When the mother and child have gone the people who have seen are free to talk. Most are disgusted and give strong judgement against the mother. The woman who has beckoned and touched and held says nothing.

*   *   *

5. Paraphernalia

And he showed me more, a little thing, the size of a
hazel nut on the palm of my hand, round like a ball.
I looked at it thoughtfully and wondered 'What is
this?' And the answer came 'It is all that is made.' I
marvelled that it continued to exist and did not
suddenly disintegrate, it was so small.

Julian of Norwich

They watched *A Winter's Tale* together on television. All else apart, Hecka found tears of relief running down her face for the lovely language in a mess of a play. Aagot followed the plot with interest, commenting on the crucial omitted scenes and the unlikely encounters and survivals. After, Hecka snuffled and talked with no view to sharing or comparing experience. Aagot didn't seem to mind, so it seemed to Hecka, but then neither did Perdita.

'The way I talk to you, I sometimes think I'd resent it very much if I was you.'

'Were.'

'Wer?'

'If I *were* you.'

'Oh. Yes. Well, proper grammar aside important like what it is . . . do you see what I mean? . . .'

'No.'

'Quite right. Faced with such a boor. It gives me a thrill when you say no; But don't you get angry with the way I behave as if I bring you into being by talking? Don't you feel like a thing in a bottle?'

'A thing?'

'A foetus, a ship, an imp, such a partial tiny thing? monosyllabic? Made from scrim?

'Scrim?'

'Shut up. Answer the question.'

'Which question?'

'Shut up. Shoddy, it's shoddy.'

'What is?'

'Scrim . . .'

'Your mind is a shambles. Ships, bottles, imps, foetuses. What a clutter.' Aagot said.

'They fall on my head, I can't help it. And my mind's not a shambles, that's a slaughter-house, and I don't kill. What do you do while I talk, listen for grammatical errors? Or phantasise that you are beating me up and gagging me?'

'Never mind what goes on in my mind. It's a lot tidier than yours, that's all.'

'That's really *all?*'

Aagot and Hecka purse up like beldams, nannies, gossips.

'It's enough for the likes of you, my girl,' says Aagot, 'An empty vessel makes the most noise.'

'And fine words butter no parsnips.'

'Least said, soonest mended.'

'Silence is golden. I prefer silver myself. I speak as I find.'

'You don't have to pick up everything you find,' says Aagot.

Hecka sees herself an old woman, soon, bundled in discards, let be by age, picking over the market leavings of cabbage leaves and squashed fruit late on Saturday afternoon, draining the orts from glasses in the public bar, making her way home with a carrier bag full of string, shirt-casings, off-cuts, firewood.

'The way I talk myself up and up until I'm silver and shattered enough to impregnate you with a shower of stars and you become pregnant with silence, the classic unwanted pregnancy. I'm like a bad writer with only enough imagination for one character and all the others are yes, no, and why women. Talking to you I'm a first-tome novelist. And good novelists have great holes in the middle of their stories. The other shapes fit around and define the vacant space, so-so. It's not like knitting.'

'Knitting?'

'Knitting. Making plain dish-cloths, no big holes. Like I do with you.'

'You make a dish-cloth out of me?'

'Could you stop being the yes, no, and why? It's very bad for my moral fibre, and it leads me into temptation. I make a rag out of you. I wish you'd stop me.'

'That's just what it feels like sometimes.'

'I thought so. Don't you mind?'

'Yes. But I like you rabbiting on.'

'*Rabbiting?* . . . You are a dish cloth. A tiny little wiper.'

'I can mop you up. Any day. You and your tiny little messes.'

'But I make a nice class of mess. Have you got any aspirin? My guts ache something rotten.'

With no hesitation Aagot answers no.

'Are you sure?'

114

'Mm. I don't use them. They are bad for you.'

'So is pain. What do you do when you've got one? Suffer nobly?'

'I don't have many pains.'

'No head-aches, period pains, tooth-ache?'

'Not much. It's better not to take drugs. The pain goes away in the end.'

'The end goes away in the pain. People die of pain.'

'Oh, that's not true.' Aagot pronounces the Ts. 'People die of illness, not pain.'

'They die because pain wears them out and the body prefers to die. My guts ache. I want aspirin, not Christian Science.'

'Haven't you got any in your bag?'

'No. Only the empty bottle. Unless there's some fallen out. Give it over, let's look.'

Aagot drags the sagging shoulder bag across the floor to Hecka. It subsides with a sigh. She takes bits from its innards and exposes them on the rug, in a circle completed by the bag. Soon they fall too thick for a circle and are flung outwards. Hecka enjoys handling what she finds. A few items have no possible use, even to her. These are chucked to the outer parts, not to be thrown away.

'If there are any they'll be right at the bottom. The top comes off those bottles they make safe for kids.'

Two diaries, this year's and last's, just in case the past is needed. Two paper-backed books, one with a pen and a bus ticket marker. Bits of paper fall out of the current diary. Hecka looks at them and lays them out:

a six month old hospital appointment card

a pay slip

a postcard of Balet's Orpheus and Euridike

old union agenda with notes handwritten on the back, used at the meeting to pass to friends and unnerve the speaker

a three-quarters-done crossword puzzle which with twenty years on a desert island would never be completed

a letter from Aagot

a scrap of paper torn from *Playboy* at the staff canteen which ends 'Great Whores are Great Artists'

'It's like a pedlar's pack,' Aagot says, 'Put it away.' She feels there is something flawed, misbegotten, uncontrolled, like a child born with its guts exposed. The midwife should have pushed them in and tidied the baby for a proper presentation to life. Hecka flaunts her abnormality and is blind to the embarrassment she causes.

'None of it's for sale, don't worry, I need it all,' she says.

a newspaper advertisement 'Feeling Feminine? 6" spiky Stilettos, Heels to 9", and a fine fetishist illustration

a group photograph of women workmates at her last job, herself, ginger dyed then, as always at the left end of the front row

a letter from a woman organising a Demeter ritual

a piece of paper covered with notes, names, phone numbers, that she has feared to discard for two years in case, you never know

a self-addressed envelope with a shopping list and a reminder among the potatoes and toilet rolls to buy Anais Nin's 'Delta of Venus'

a wodge of invitations to a past Christmas party

a dole office attendance card

'How can you need all that?'

'I do. I've forgotten why, but I do,' Aagot wishes she would put all this stuff, stuffing, away.

no aspirins

an envelope with two cheque books, two paying-in books, one of each dead, alive

used tissues, and clean ones: she shakes them and a white tablet falls out. It is a peppermint and she dusts and eats it.

a bottle of cologne for her hair and arm-pits and neck when she's out and suspects she smells

lip salve

the empty aspirin bottle

a tape measure

'Why?' asks Aagot.

'I forget.'

a purse bulging with small change and disused keys

two boxes of matches

five packets of cigarette papers

116

two tampax, one out of its wrapper, the two halves lost from
each other
an unfilled kidney donor card (Hecka would give her kidneys
and her corneas but fears that at a hint her nearest, who are
not all her dearest, would glady donate her whole body to be
played with by young male medical students.)
a can tag
a watch strap
bus tickets
a pen-knife
a base of tobacco shreds
no aspirin

The side pockets give up pens, combs, scissors, elasto-
plast, library tickets, drawing pins, chalks and a thick felt tip
pen for graffiti, another peppermint, and two aspirins.
Hecka sits happy at the centre of her providence. She picks
over the entrails with satisfaction and crows over the aspirins.
'It's all here.'
Aagot looks at the stuffing laid out over and beyond the rug.
She is discomforted by an indecent act, a wallowing.

'The only thing missing is a brown paper bag to put over
my head if the bomb falls.'

'Get in the bag, it already looks like a fall-out shelter.'

'What've you got?' Hecka asks, looking at Aagot's small
shoulder pouch.

'Money, keys, a handkerchief.'

'Show.'
Affectionate, long-suffering, she undoes her bag. Money,
keys, a handkerchief.

'You know what you carry with you?'

'Of course I do. Don't you?'

'Of course I don't. Is one pound fifty all you've got?'

'No. the rest is at home. I knew I wouldn't need much
when I came out.'

'How? How can you know that? How can you tell what
you'll need? Anything can happen.'

'No it can't. I know I won't need an unfilled kidney donor
card or a dead cheque book or a broken tampax or three
combs or a penknife . . . .'

117

'Lay off. Lay off my life.' Hecka is stuffing the bag full again. 'Lay off naming my things. Why haven't you got paraphernalia like me? All women have paraphernalia.'

'I own things, if that's what you mean.'

'I know. You've got a place to live and some books and clothes and cups and plates, but that's property.'

'All right. I have property. I don't carry bits and pieces around with me.'

'They are bits and pieces of me. I'm not safe without them.'

'But half of them are useless, or dead, or pointless' says Aagot.

'Then so am I.'

'Why do you need last year's diary? And three combs?'

'This here diary contains names and addresses I could use to undermine the State. And the three combs are in case I lose two.'

'But you're not going to undermine the State. Or lose two combs.'

Hecka is wailing and hugging her bag. 'I might. How can I know? I might.'

'I know what I am and what I'm doing.'

Hecka is startled. Aagot's voice and gaze are fierce in their precision.

'I don't. They might take my property from me at any time, but they'll leave me my bag of bits because I'm a woman. I don't understand. You travel and I don't, but you don't protect yourself.'

'You don't need to. Travelling is safe. You are provided for.'

Again, the excess clip of class and conviction.

'Aagot, are you sure?'

'Yes.'

'Don't you think every morning when you leave the house you must carry your things with you because the day might end with you in prison or in hell?'

'Of course not. That's paranoid. Don't say that.'

'Don't say that to me. It makes me sure I'm persecuted.'

*   *   *

118

Hecka put up with the common stock dream of finding herself in a strange town lost, having a destination imposed on her and being unable to find the way. The expected street would not be there; instead, a wall, a barricade of traffic with no gaps. There was no bus stop or she had missed the bus. She would find herself off the road, trying to climb backyard fences to make her way to the road she could see between the houses, but not reach. All the time she was getting later, not for some chosen meeting but a dutiful appointment. She usually awoke to a grey exhaustion aware that the dream was exactly a paradigm of the day, that it was an official brown envelope with instructions, the last of which was that she would fail to perform them.

One night in bed with Aagot the same form of dream presented itself, changed. She was in a strange town, but this time on her way home by coach. At her request the coach stopped: stop here please for half an hour. The other passengers were pleased. They got off and she walked slowly along an unfamiliar street in an unknown town, looking in the shop windows which were full of bits and pieces, necklaces, bracelets, soaps, shampoos, soft toys. She saw each thing very clearly as familiar. She had her shoulder bag with money and all she needed. There was no anxiety about the passing of time, no fear the coach would not be there when she wanted it. She had a friend in the town, and the street was a turning just ahead of her on the same side of the road, no standing at the curb, hopeless, trying to cross a busy road, no sense of appointed time running out. She turned into the side street and knew which house she wanted, she saw it, orange brick and laurel bush, and walked towards it expecting welcome.

She woke and made love to Aagot as if that were the fulfillment of the dream.

*   *   *

Hecka's birthday, and Aagot was away. A parcel arrived. First, string knots. Then cellotaped brown paper. Inside, a plastic sandwich box with a tight lid: inside, a lining of green moss: inside, hundreds of snowdrops.

119

Hecka picked out and looked at every green and white flower and set them in all the small jars she could find. She emptied two paste pots when she'd used all the egg cups. Some floated in pudding bowls. For two weeks she gave them drops of fresh water each day. When Aagot returned there was one yellow egg cup holding the last six flowers.

She pressed the moss into the ground in the garden. She kept the lunch box and folded the brown paper and put it in a drawer.

She knew then that she would never again be given such a gift.

Hecka's gift to Aagot was a silver chain, a gift corrupted by the greater pleasure she would enjoy from seeing Aagot wearing it than any pleasure Aagot would have from receiving it. Hecka apologised implicitly by giving it in a paper bag. She began to understand the alternative convention of thanking the receiver for accepting your gift. Aagot wore the necklace but often took it off in Hecka's presence, saying that it chafed. She always removed it if Hecka touched it when they made love. It carried a taint.

*   *   *

They walked up a hill path. On the way Aagot had been explaining her experience of being a Christian and how her feminist reading had made sense of her discomfort, even unhappiness, in the Church. Reading had given her support to move away from what she now saw as a male oppressive institution which could only degrade her and tell her lies. It wasn't easy for Aagot to explain this much. Hecka didn't help: she asked Aagot what she had looked at while the service was going on, what she had confessed, whether she felt guilty for her sins, loved the Virgin Mary, and had talked to the nuns when she received instruction.

Hecka listened from the moment Aagot used the word 'unhappiness', and stumbled amongst the huge slow abstractions for some small sharp bits she could feel the shape of.

Aagot wasn't happy either. She spoke in answer to Hecka's questions as if it were an unimportant subject and yet it lowered her spirits to be pressed for account and detail. Hecka's starting point, Aagot's unhappiness, was the wrong one to free her to speak. Again their talk set them further from each other.

At the top of the hill there was a small dark wood. The path went in. They kissed in the shelter of old trees and walked. The imprint of a rider was weathered into the ground. White wind-flowers grew. It was very quiet.

A copper coloured fox crossed the path in front of them. It stopped to look at them and went on unafraid. Hecka thought it was a dog until she saw the golden brown brush.

'It's a fox . . .' she said. She had never seen a real one before. 'It didn't care about us. It didn't care. Did you see?'

'Yes,' Aagot said, and told of a friend of hers who worked with an anti-blood sports group to disrupt hunting. She described the custom of smearing the youngest member of the hunt with the animal's blood and giving the brush to the victor. It sounded unhygienic, in the telling.

'It didn't care,' said Hecka.

On the way back down the hill Hecka turned to face Aagot and ran backwards. The path was deeply rutted and steep. She knew she wouldn't hurt herself. She looked at the sky and the ground and still thinking of belief in gods she said

'I do. He's up there. It belongs to him, all that. She's down here. All this is Hers.'

Aagot was smiling at her and the level horizon line of earth and sky behind her.

'It doesn't fit,' Hecka said, 'the sky. The colours are wrong. There are no names for the shapes, only clouds. The names for the things down here are old and endless.'

Out of breath she stopped. The land and sky held still and clear as a child's painting, simplified, a telegram of landscape, an idea. The sky was plain strong blue. The land was shapely, grey with flints, green with young crops. Behind a gorse bush burned yellow and sepia. Aagot standing was as notional and as solid as the flints.

'I love you,' Hecka said and turned bluntly away. At her feet was a bunch of wind-flowers someone had dropped.

They were dying. She picked them up and put them on her coat.

'They're dead,' Aagot said.

'I know. They're my trophy. I'm not a good hunter.'

*   *   *

How much time they spent in churches, neither of them being faithful. There were proper reasons. It was common ground. There was time to waste before they arrived at final destinations. Often they could have walked in a park or window-shopped, but Aagot's feet led the way to tabernacles, chapels, churches high and low. Some were places she had been taken to herself, for culture and instruction, when she was young. They visited a cathedral city: what else to do there than enter its centre, neither inclined to a Marxist gesture?

And there was the Catholic church Aagot went to as a girl, for a while, alone, and as a strange gift allowed Hecka into.

Hecka did not take her to churches. Hecka took her to standing stones, pubs, mounds, cafes, ancient paths, to hospital to visit Mrs. Harris. Hecka, as May, said that Aagot was a friend. Aagot looked aside as the peculiar talk went and did not comment even on Hecka's change of name. Lily was off duty. She and Aagot never met.

Aagot took Hecka to churches. Every church has the oldest, smallest, most improbable something. Cromwell did or didn't smash the glass, or break the stone noses. You are invited to wonder that it did or didn't happen. Ministers leave pamphlets telling you so next to boxes for the fifty pence it costs to keep the church open for you to admire. You grope for fifty pence and admiration, it is rarely awe; you come to see the sights, not to see sights. The bell tower is made of wood, wonder that it has stood for hundreds of years when we know domestic sheds and frames rot in no time at all, and murmur craftsmanship, what became of it. A stone floor slopes, look up, the whole structure leans its weight on marshy ground, how has it stood against all the weight of time? Time, and time again: a chance scrape at plaster twenty

122

years ago reveals, revealed, ochre painting and words from six hundred years ago. The essayist or poet mentioned the church in a minor work. The painter probably sat here. This may be where the marriage took place. Tradition has it that near this spot. In the plague. After the Reformation. The ruins of the Precinct wall. All the lovely graveyards, a new flower potted on a seventeenth century grave, who, why? Small grass mounds more defiantly owned and named by the dead than the miniature patios with paving, rails and carved claims.

Hecka wanted to be loved by her for ever and ever, so be it, all shall be well, and all shall be well, and all manner of things shall be well, but it was already too late, she was a pile of grass, she was looking at her future, Aagot took and persistently showed her, as it shall be, so it is. Hecka was happy for her future, it was being urged that there was the trouble.

They sat in London churches and idled through hymn books vying for remembered words. They had in common girlhoods of school assembly, the Lord's Prayer and muted singing. They both remembered the boredom and sticky warmth, the essential smell of blood and heat in a crowded room.

Tourists walking by as they sat, visitors hushed in the nave or the aisle and stepped the special heel-toe creep of respect. People who sit in a church are in higher standing then those who walk about. Hecka wondered only at the stillness, the good behaviour of everything, especially the flowers in brass pots, they shone, they did not seem to be dying as cut flowers die. She watched them closely and they flared. Aagot was a sight-seer, Hecka was not. Aagot took the pamphlets and went to look at the oldest, smallest, and most improbable. She left Hecka in peace, was always very good at leaving her alone and then Hecka valued her as a companion. It left her free to sit and blur, believing as she did that revelation comes if at all from inertia, lack of occupation anyway; Aagot thinking that life is for living, which is occupied. Mostly Hecka got maudlin and watched the flowers with narrowed eyes, and Aagot collected things, items of information, what else Hecka didn't know because Aagot didn't say.

Hecka didn't collect. She couldn't remember which was the oldest, the oddest, held the most infamous dead. She loved them all, the click of the iron latch always the same sound, the cool still air, the surety of a cross, wooden seats and stone, the right to sit uselessly not thinking. She could sit and not think for a long time, until Aagot had seen with her delicate eye all the delicacies, and Hecka had almost seen nothing.

Sometimes Hecka cried. She found dark corners to do it in. Mush, slush, she said, give over.

Do you love me Aagot?

Do you love me?

Do you?

I wait for the cock to crow.

She cried for her sins and for a longing for grace.

She knew what she meant. Aagot didn't mind. Hecka was discreet. Tourists crept a little the more respectfully, presuming her to be bereaved, which she was, she was.

What I am trying to find out is: why did Aagot take her to churches? She professed rejection of all dogma and all concepts of the Spirit moving, was fierce about the silliness of sin and goodness. She was interested but cold to the generations who built and came to plead, grieve, hate, confess and worship, this last word one which glazed her eyes. She seemed to lay churches as she collected rubber stamps in her passport. Greece was done and so was Canterbury cathedral.

What I am trying to find out is: why did she take Hecka to bed?

In Canterbury Cathedral Hecka sat near the back of the vast lop-sided city and over a tannoy which needed a new speaker listened to a reading about Doubting Thomas, and it was specially for her, as everything really is, or isn't: the acceptance of either as true makes you mad. Then it was. But she said to herself it's no good, you gave it to Thomas, let him touch and be sure, and you gave it to a few others on roads or in rooms, then you stopped. She was surrounded by red and gold patterns, musical form, signs and symbols like all the stories ever written which say things are shapely, you can look any novel in the eye and it will return your gaze with the

124

yes of conviction or the convicted liar. She wanted to touch the flesh. It's just a story. It's all there is.

She sat alone and cried very decently. Rows in front of her a little girl had been lifted from her pushchair and sat next to her guardian on the hard wooden seat. Something, everything about the place was too much for the child. She hung her head and began to wail quietly. She was already well trained. Her voice was small but through the organ and the choral Hecka heard her: I want my mummy. At three years old most of her anguish was at the breakdown of decorum. Oh dear. I want my mummy. She cried quietly with her head down ashamed. Oh dear. Her guardian put her in the pushchair and took her out. Hecka cried for the girl and for herself, like an idiot child.

She remembered then three most beautiful things which had been done. One, a gift of small white flowers in midwinter, unexpected, grace, a shock, she would never be the same. You shouldn't go upsetting a lifetime's work at shaping up like that. Two, holding someone she loved while she died and when the spasms ceased but she was still unconscious, the woman turned her face transformed into such sweetness Hecka had never seen before and never would again in this world and kissed her. A nurse had led Hecka away persuading her with difficulty that the woman was dead. Three, standing in the Lady chapel of a cathedral crypt, the fragile silver grey ancient vulnerable enduring stone shelter on which the massive weight of the whole cathedral pressed and the little stronghold full of holes bore it, the white lilies fading, the niche for her statue empty, the silver cross thin as fingers. Because of these and others she had been too stupid to remember she would never be the same.

Aagot took Hecka to the church in south London which she had begun entering when her mother died. She didn't tell her grandmother what she was doing of course, words were fouled and dangerous. Her grandmother knew, but said nothing when Aagot rose early on Sunday mornings and walked out without breakfast. If it was not spoken of then it was not exactly happening. Hecka loved her so dearly when she took her to the end of the ugly road where she had lived and pointed to the window of her flat. She feared to take her any nearer. Hecka loved her so much and feared that any word would trample and crush. She let Hecka near and it was dangerous and Aagot was sick and frightened. She walked her to the church and Hecka expected some majesty, at least some gloss and shine, but it was a modernist red brick square block, with two spruce trees each side of a gravel path, trimmed grass. It could have been a clinic, a small council office. She hesitated to go in and Hecka waited on her permission. Inside, blunt chairs in rows, a smell of pine furniture polish, on the walls the Stations of the Cross painted to deter indulgence in passion, a modern stained glass window behind a plain altar. It was, Aagot said, excitement and colour to her when she was young; grey star perhaps in a black sky. Hecka could not heal such mutilation any more than Aagot could heal hers. Aagot forgave her, as Hecka never forgave Aagot, for not turning water into wine.

*　　　　*　　　　*

Hecka set out to spend the night with Aagot. Knowing she was going there that evening gave a lightness to her whole working day. She skimmed across it and was nice to the people she met. She saw them receive it, and loved Aagot the more as her source. From late afternoon she began to get ready. She washed, and started to count hours. She laid out on the bed the things she would need.

Freeze there and look: there is something wrong. Clean underclothes for the morning, yes, purse, and a feminist book borrowed to return. Missing: sleeping pills, shawl, her own book and papers, beer cans, diary, crossword puzzle: insurances. She had not provided for herself for such a journey except with a smile and a feeling that everything was beautiful, even herself. She was well on the way to mouthing the convinced statement of the rapist: 'I love you'; she forgot the vices of passion.

She combed her hair, improved her eyebrows, put on new black gear with acid yellow ornaments. The clothes were tight. Wherever they pressed she felt majestic. She was already raised up and proud. Witless. If she had her wits, knew what was going to happen, she would have carried her fragments, her bag of bones and nostrums, crossword puzzle to give her words to beat down so that she would leave Aagot alone, sleeping pills for indifference, her shawl to hug herself in when she felt the cold, which was fear, which made her dangerous.

She imagined herself insubstantially to be moving towards real life, being on earth in her body, and safe. She forgot that this is the most dangerous moment of all, when imagination runs ahead of journeys, words, and all intervening acts. Her eyes and appetites were huge and limpid, stupid as an ox chewing in expectation of food, on its way to the slaughter house, smelling too late blood and fear and trampling panic.

She was going to her lover, that's all, come, come.

As she walked the hundred yards from the bus stop to the house she smelled and knew. What moved her and had equivalence to her delight all day was vile. The sprawling generosity she had felt was the opening of a cage, the killer's belief that he will be good now that the world unlocks and is available to his reprieve, he would not dream of killing again. He does. The world makes a ritual gesture of admission, no more, it cannot, it is fragile. It is not enough and the killer does again what he knows best how to do.

Aagot opened the door.

All rooms belong to somebody, so they are safe or risky, never neutral. Aagot's door, passage, stairs and living room were hers; from the gate hot, hot, getting cool, cooler, cold, cold.

On one of Hecka's early visits, when simple questions could be asked, she had looked around the room and said 'Where are your things, Aagot?'

'Oh, it's in a terrible mess.'

There was no nightdress discarded, cardigans, shopping bags, cosmetics, pens, biscuits, used cups, tissues, bits of paper lying around because they evaded pigeon-holes, no drifts of dust at the edges of shelves, no traces of anything in the doing. There was a surprising amount of absence.

'Where's the mess?'

'I haven't hoovered for a week. I've been mending my jeans and forgot to put the sewing box away.'

'Where does it usually go?'

'In the bottom of the cabinet, on the left. And those cushions are supposed to be put away in that corner until night time.'

Her room was under control. One book was read at a time, the others were under glass, books on chemistry, mathematics and feminism. Intrusive as it was, Hecka used to take them out to look at. They had their dust-covers and were not scribbled on at all. Some were in Norwegian, which was an effective barrier to prying. When Aagot was out of the room Hecka looked through the desk slats where letters were kept; in one section, work contracts, in another, insurance papers and passport, in another three recent letters to be answered. She wondered where the immortelles were. A serviceable long-life plant held still as a table. The colours were fawn and quiet green. It gave very little away.

There were oddities: that the fire was never lit in anticipation of her coming, but always with the labour of paper wood and coal, after her arrival, although she always came to appointment; that the comfortable chair was always far from the fire and had to be moved nearer for warmth, involving Hecka in the labour of moving it herself or asking if she could; that the kettle for making coffee in the room was kept on the floor in a corner behind a small table, needing a steep reach and a walk across the room to a power point if coffee were asked for or offered.

Privacy has many facets and holds in many desires, including the desire to be breached. Aagot wanted to be persuaded into offering comfort and welcome. Hecka knew nothing about persuasion. She chose to see only the exclusion, the visible irksomeness of being provided for. A slip of a sigh, a frown on Aagot's face, and Hecka would find it hard to breathe the air because the air in that room belonged to Aagot.

She had been in the house for three quarters of an hour without taking off her coat and scarf. She kept her bag close

128

to her side and sat on a hard chair far back from the fire. She needed to be made welcome, did not know why. She wanted Aagot to say I love you come in, come, I'm glad you're early take the paper I'll make you coffee now, come. It was as if her arrival was a pleasure to Aagot but her presence was not. Months later she began to understand. At that time though her own behaviour puzzled her and scared Aagot into refinement and retreat. Hecka picked up a bit of ash which had fallen from her cigarette and put it in the ashtray. She brushed the remaining flecks to remove all traces of infringement. She wanted to be welcomed, and wasn't, and wrongly took that to mean that she wasn't welcome.

When talk failed Hecka said 'What shall we do this evening?' She had already lost what she wanted, to be wondered at in her new gear, told she looked lovely, given words of love, and then to spend the evening and the night in splendour. To talk was next best, but Aagot was tired and low-spirited.

'Let's talk,' said Aagot, and leaned back and waited.

'Yes.' Hecka said.

'Well?'

'Is there something special?'

'No. I just think we should talk more.'

'Yes.'

'Well?' Aagot said.

'Give us a clue. I can't do it by numbers. What do you fancy talking about?'

'Anything you like.'

A ticking began in Hecka's head. There was a short time limit before something nasty would happen if she didn't come up with what was wanted.

'What's your favourite colour?' she asked.

'Blue, I think.'

'What's your favourite time of day?'

'Um . . . the afternoon.'

'What's your favourite food?'

'I don't know.'

'What animals do you like best?'

'Um . . . Look, what is this?'

'I don't know. I thought you might ask me something.'

'This isn't what people mean by talk,' said Aagot.

'No.'

'You're not up to it, are you?'

'No,' said Hecka truly. 'Let's play cards.'

'I haven't got any.'

'I saw some in the kitchen last time I was here.'

'They shouldn't be in the kitchen.'

Aagot went to look. Hecka sat and worried. She was in trouble and couldn't understand. Aagot came back.

'What should we play then?' she asked.

'Poker?'

'I don't know it.'

'Blackjack?'

'No.'

Time was still running out.

'Snap? I'm good at that.'

'No.'

'Beggar My Neighbour?'

'What's that?'

Hecka explained the simple game of winning by picking up the collective heap, laying four cards for an ace, three for a king, two for a queen and one for a jack. She dealt. They laid. Aagot won the first game. She had picked up on the deal three aces and, most useful for winning, all the jacks. With a jack you stand the best chance of picking up a thick pile of cards.

'Let's play again,' Aagot said.

Aagot dealt. Again she had the four jacks. The game took longer, Hecka felt herself fighting back, but still Aagot won.

'What did you say it's called?'

'Beggar My Neighbour. Or Beggar My Neighbour Out of Doors.'

'Why?'

'I suppose because you strip the other player bit by bit of all she has until all she has is one card and that's taken too.'

'I like it,' Aagot said, 'It's not a game of skill, but I like it.'

Hecka dealt. Aagot had the four jacks and three queens, two kings and three aces, and won.

'I'm not so sure it's not a game of skill,' Hecka said.

'Why? It just depends on the deal. A computer could tell you the result of you fed in the facts of the deal.'

They played once more. Aagot won. Hecka did not even pick up once. 'This is peculiar,' she said.

'Why? It can only be chance. By the laws of chance if we played enough games we'd win and lose equally.'

'It has something to do with you,' Hecka said.

'How can it be? I can't influence chance. It's all in the lie of the cards . . .'

'I want to try something. Just once. No, twice. You deal, and we won't play.'

Aagot shuffled and dealt. Hecka spread out and examined the cards in two neutral heaps. Aagot's hand had no jacks, one ace, one king. Hecka had all the rest of the winning cards. Then Hecka shuffled and dealt. Again she spread out the two uncontending heaps. She had four jacks, two aces, four kings, and a queen. Aagot had only two aces and three queens.

'It's just chance, there you are,' said Aagot.

'But we're not playing.'

'So?'

'When we're not playing I could win, when we are I'm not likely to.'

'That's mathematical nonsense. If we went on dealing long enough it would even out. It's nothing to do with whether we take each other on or not.'

Hecka puzzled. 'How many times would we have to deal before the cards showed they're impartial?'

'They're impartial all the time.'

'But it doesn't seem like it. They seem to have a bias.'

'They can't have. You'd see in the end. You can't tell until it happens. And each deal has a fifty-fifty chance for either of us holding a winning hand.'

'It doesn't seem so.'

'You've just got two runs which were probably winners. It levels.'

'But we weren't playing. One more game?'

Aagot dealt. As she reached to pick up and compact her cards

Hecka put a hand over hers and exchanged the two heaps. Aagot won. Hecka's last card was the ace of spades; she picked up six cards on the strength of it, and lost them all.

The evening and the night were filled with absurd and painful performances in which Hecka begged to be led away from a spotlight where she was confined to a mime of distress. The circle of darkness around her held her in a prison cell, an interrogation chamber, a dock; places where you are compelled to speak, or act, but confined by codes of what cannot be said or done. The result is hysteria, theatre, bedlam.

Aagot had taken a series of snapshots of Hecka in her own house, talking, drinking tea, laughing. Hecka saw the prints for the first time this evening in Aagot's presence and waited for words of kindness about her appearance. The words did not come, as why should they. Hecka loved the pictures and was surprised to be pleased with images of herself, but getting no word, requested scissors and cut off the strips of herself. Scissors cut paper. She tore them roughly in pieces and threw them into the fire.

'I don't like them. I don't like images of myself. I don't like to see how ugly I am. You can do better than that for yourself.'

'I quite like them,' said Aagot, rigid, watching. Stone blunts scissors. She gave very little away. Hecka brought forward to the centre of the mantelpiece two other photographs, one of Aagot and one of a friend of hers.

'Now, that's nice, isn't it.' It ripped and hurt like a slow burn to destroy the pictures of herself. Fire burns paper.

They talked a little over a long time of work and work politics. Austen meets Bronte and both are baffled. Hecka was bestial with irritation at the sound of Aagot's voice picking and refined with fear. She realised that she never stuttered when she was talking to Aagot as she did with friends and people at work. Her confidence was awful. It was the confidence that she could dwindle Aagot by striking her with words, or equally well by listening to her, dumbfounding her. She cried later to be free from the arrogance of judging language: she crowed with pride in judging it.

Aagot began to prepare the bed. The small divan had to be

dismantled, blankets fetched, sheets laid out. Hecka offered coldly to sleep on the floor next to the divan so that Aagot could get a good night's rest. Aagot's movements truly suggested that a fragile and necessary order was being upset, and that she was truly weary and despairing. Hecka refused to make the act of love, to override this distress. She colluded with it and made it potent. Aagot had not commented on her new black gear with the acid yellow ornaments. Aagot had not over-ridden with passion. She held passive, not knowing or enabled to do what was asked of her, presented with a mirror in which to see her chilliest and most limited self.

They lay down for the night. Hecka wanted to be forgiven and welcomed. It was a bit too late. She put an arm across to touch, but Aagot was stone, or half asleep. She slept easily as she always did. Hecka cursed that she had no sleeping tablets and no candle. The circle of light was gone, the darkness invaded her totally. If she had a candle, a night-light, she could sit and smoke, think and watch Aagot sleeping. She was lovely to keep watch by.

Hecka sat up on cushions and inched her coat on for warmth, moving as little as possible. The curtains shut out the street lights. The house was silent, the darkness full of folds and poisonous. She remembered a night alone in a bed and breakfast room; when she had switched off the light the room was dense with hair, matted and stifling, unbreathable, the room belonged to it. She had tried several times and had spent the night sitting up with the light on.

The house was silent, the darkness full of folds. In it human voices began to quarrel and squeal like pigs. She was surrounded with malice and argument. A voice suddenly shouted rage: she contracted, and sure that Aagot heard the voice, that it broke her sleep, said she was sorry. The voices were coarse and stupid, charged with spite. They muttered and shrilled hatred for each other. Each time one voice broke fury Hecka asked forgiveness from Aagot for them. She brought them into being, though they did not seem to be part of herself. They were certainly not locked in sleep. They existed in the thick folds, inside and around. Hecka was badly frightened. The night was too cold for her to go and sit in the kitchen. She wished very much she had a car to get home in. Aagot slept.

There was a lull. The attackers were leaving. Hecka rested her head and began to sleep.

A crackling, an electric cracking, an impossible sound, a séance presence, began. It moved, had no exact place, was not a human voice. Hecka couldn't recognise it as anything known or possible. She had no defence against terror except that of a child. She put her head under the cover and cried, wailed for help. 'There's something, please listen, there's something in the room.'

Aagot woke and listened. It cracked. 'No there isn't,' she said. Hecka convulsed with fear. 'I hear it. Listen. Please. There's something.' Hecka was sobbing.

Aagot put the light on. 'It's only Annie.'

With the light on and Aagot awake Hecka could look out. Annie the house cat had slipped in and was playing with a piece of cellophane. Aagot carried the cat out and threw the cellophane away. The light went off.

'It was only the cat.'

'You said it was nothing.'

'Well, it was only the cat.'

'You said you couldn't hear anything.'

'I didn't.'

Did she mean she hadn't said that, or that she hadn't heard a sound? Why hadn't she heard, or why did she say she hadn't? Aagot was rolled away towards sleep. There was no asking. Hecka snuffled because of her tears, using her sleeve and was very tired. At the same time she needed to go to the lavatory. She crept out without disturbing Aagot. For some time she sat cold but safe in total light. She forgot that dark was just at her back coming in through the small window. She slept a while sitting there. Her eyes opened when she heard small thuds. She was prepared now for gross insanity, her punishment, not her making. At her feet several wasps were crawling. Another thudded into her back. A small rain of them beat against the half-open window behind her, and more came in. They were yellow and black, winged, crawling, aiming for the light she had given herself. She had brought them into the house and they were real. If she held still perhaps they would cover her and she would be discovered for what she was. But she went to the back room and closed the window against a thudding mob of them. Like the voices they persisted, were massed, and were hostile. Many were already inside the room. Perhaps there were other openings to Aagot's house through which she was summoning them in. She had to tell Aagot because it was dangerous, a whole nest on the move with burning stings. She crept back to the room and touched Aagot's shoulder, in her sleep Aagot said 'No.'

'Aagot. Aagot, there are wasps, lots of wasps coming in. I'm sorry.'

'No there aren't.'

'There are. There really are. In the lavatory and the back room. I don't know where else. Thousands.'

By her 'really' she accepted the madness of the voices and the cat crack. Aagot rose and checked the windows of the house. She got down into bed again.

'There are wasps, aren't there.'

'Yes.'

Hecka went to sleep. It was greying to dawn. She woke at half past eight, instantly. She clambered up convinced it was a working day and that she was making Aagot late for work by lying there. Aagot had gone. Hecka pulled on her clothes, stuffed her bag, rebuilt the divan, folded the bedding, tidied away, gradually remembering it was Sunday, still impelled to remove every trace of her presence there, except herself. Aagot must have heard. She came in just as Hecka was finishing.

'Do you want some coffee?'

'No, no, it's all right.'

Aagot stretched. 'I slept well. It was lovely.'

*   *   *

Water quenches fire
Fire melts scissors
Scissors cut paper
Paper wraps stone

Stone withstands fire
Fire burns paper
Water soaks paper
Water rusts scissors
Stone blunts scissors
Stone dams water

Stone withstands fire. Neither wins. Fire goes out but stone stands scorched.

*   *   *

'I've mislaid that necklace,' Aagot said.

'What necklace?' Aagot was wearing the thick silver chain she had bought herself, and the blue beads which her last lover had given her.

'You know.'

'No ... Do you mean the one I gave you? You lost it?' Hecka felt an insidious pain. Aagot yawned and stretched.

'Mm. Perhaps I dropped it at home.'

'Have you looked?'

'I couldn't see it lying around.'

Hecka, lying around, made a strong effort not to disappear.

'Where else could it be?'

'I might have left it here. Have you seen it?'

'No. I'll look.' She stood up and moved to the bed to lift the cloth fall of the bed cover. That would be the most likely, since she had not seen it on any surfaces, that it had been dropped and concealed under the folds when Aagot had taken it off, merely removed it, found it chafing, or whatever.

'Make me some coffee, will you,' said Aagot.

'You've got some.'

'It's gone cold.'

Hecka went to the kitchen with a hurt that was beyond accounting for. She heard the bump of books, scraping of a chair, opening and closing of drawers while she stood waiting in the kitchen. She felt absurdly that she had been ordered off-stage for reason of plot and half expected a call: you can come back now. The noises were theatrical. She found

136

herself humming and rinsing clean cups, performing un-awareness of intrigue.

They send you out of the room, and whisper, and move things. They call you back into silence and two are seated on an improvised long throne covered with a cloth. They wear paper crowns and solemnly invite you to kneel and take vows and sit between the king and queen, a ceremony of accept-ance; but mischief is in the air. You sit in the vacant centre of the throne and the cloth gives way, there is no solid seat under you and you fall on your arse and the solemnity renders into yells of glee; you had taken it seriously: who would enthrone you?

When she came back Aagot was sitting ceremoniously on a chair, arms resting Solomon-wise.

'I've looked.'

'Perhaps it's at your place then.'

'I don't think so.'

The tone had the finality of No.

'Please look though.'

'Of course I will, what do you think I am?' It was a spurt of anger. Hecka couldn't understand why she was taken to think anything bad, anyone could be careless, mislay some-thing of value. She drank and talked about other things while she began her own search, knowing her own room and its crevices better than Aagot did. She bent again to look at the dusty floor under the bed.

'It's not there,' Aagot said firmly. 'I've looked everywhere. I'm sure it's not there. Leave it, it will turn up.'

Hecka went to open the japanned box where she kept her beads and such.

'What's that?' Aagot asked.

'It's my bead box.'

'It's not there, I've looked.'

'But if you didn't know what it is . . .'

'I forgot for a moment. Why are you making so much fuss?'

'I don't know. I'm sorry. I suppose it's the only lasting thing I've given you.'

'Well, it's gone. For now, I mean. It will turn up. Things do.'

'Do they?'

Hecka shivered.

'What's the matter?'

'Nothing. Someone walked over my grave.'

'And what is that supposed to mean?'

Why was Aagot so angry?

'Supposed? It's just an old saying. If you shiver and feel cold for no reason, someone is walking over the ground where you'll be buried.'

'Hardly reasonable is it. Morbid.'

'It's just an old saying. For frights.'

'What have *you* got to be frightened about?'

'I don't know. Some people say it's an angel flying overhead.'

Her face down to her cup, Hecka missed the play of expression on Aagot's face.

'Could we stop talking about you, and death, and angels? None of it makes sense.'

Hecka knew then she had present cause to be frightened.

'OK.'

Silence.

'Well?' Aagot said, 'What are you sulking about?'

'I'm not sulking.'

'You're the talker, what have you got to say?'

A flick of courage, and Hecka asked 'What am I on trial for?'

'What nonsense. I'm just trying to talk to you and you make all this fuss about angels and death and trials. You make it impossible. You are impossible to talk to.'

'Don't say that.'

'It's true.'

'It's a sentence of death.'

'I tell you a simple fact, a few simple words, and you say it's a death sentence. It's just a fact.'

At last Hecka was sure she was being finely worked over and had something to be punished for. If she could endure it she might find out. She had no choice, she knew very clearly that she did not want Aagot to leave, did not want again to find herself alone in the room bewildered and unexpressed.

'About the necklace,' she said. Aagot gave a pucker of

138

irritation. ' . . . Perhaps you took it off in your bathroom. It could be there.'

'You really think I'm stupid, don't you? That I'd do something like that? I told you. I've looked. It's not in my place.' Hecka was confused. A few minutes ago she had the impression it could be in Aagot's house, but that she hadn't troubled to look carefully. Now it wasn't possible at all.

'I must have left it here. You've put it somewhere,' Aagot said.

'I think I'd remember.'

'You forget everything. You don't remember what happened two hours ago.'

'Why, what happened two hours ago?'

Aagot shouted. 'Stop making fun of me.'

Silence.

'I'm not. I'm not having any fun.'

'Oh yes you are, at my expense.'

'Permit me to know. The last thing I'm having is fun.'

'All this fuss about a necklace. It's got to be here.'

'But you've looked and I've looked and it's not.'

'It must be. It's the only reasonable answer.'

'All right. Forget it. I'll look after you've gone.'

'It's not important then? Suddenly, it's not important? I haven't looked properly? You can see things I can't see?'

'I'm afraid . . .'

'*You're* afraid . . .'

'Maybe . . .'

'Don't commit yourself to yes or no . . .'

'I can. I don't want to. I want to see what you see. Forgive me.'

'Oh, but *I'm* deaf dumb blind and stupid. And I don't know how to talk. I don't see angels hovering in the air and graves opening under my feet. I think I'm talking and I'm told it's a trial.'

Hecka panicked. She began to search the litter basket. If only the trinket could be found, the palmed silver held up to prove: paper and matchboxes fell onto the floor. Aagot eased, Hecka did not know why.

'How trivial you are. You look really silly. If you could see yourself.'

'I can.'

'You can see yourself but not a little silver chain? And you expect me to take you seriously?'

At the bottom of the bin, holding a crumpled paper, and with shock after the words, Hecka asked

'Where is it Aagot?'

Aagot was enraged.

'You really think I've got it? I'm playing games like you do? I've got your nasty little chain?'

Hecka walked blind into the middle of the room and moved towards the bookshelf where she hadn't searched. Aagot shouted 'Stop. Stop making fun of me.'

A steel gate fell in front of Hecka. She had to step back to catch her balance as the barrier crashed. She came and sat as near to Aagot as she dared.

'Let's forget it. As you say, it will turn up.'

'So I had to go through all this before you see reason. And now when you've had your fun you tell me to forget it?'

'I haven't had any fun.'

'Then what do you get out of it, doing this to me?'

It was hopeless, nothing to be gained, nothing lost.

'Aagot. I really think you are doing something to me too.'

Hecka knew this was terminal outrage. Aagot left. She wept all the way as she drove home with a terrible urgency, and fell asleep as soon as she went to bed.

Hecka was dry and ice-cold. She jumbled on old sweaters and scarves and drank coffee and wished for liquor or drugs. She found herself walking round the cluttered room fingering things and realised she was still searching. There seemed to be strong reason to, against all reason. She lifted the edges of the carpet and moved the bed away from the wall. First wildly then with care she felt through the drawers of clothes, crumpling and shaking each garment. She poked into the pockets of trousers and jackets hanging up even though the trouser pockets were upside down and couldn't have held anything. She scarcely knew what she was searching for, something elusive, invisible, of gross importance, and it would be worse when she found it. More coffee, and she emptied her shoulder bag, stripped the bed, felt into the vamp of every shoe.

She knew. When the house was quiet, the last dog barked, the last car faded, all babies slept, and she was in the speaking silence, she blundered towards the high bookshelf. She heard the steel door crash and backed away. Because it was hopeless if she did and if she did not, she walked through. A wall ghost, it let her. Ritually she began at the top shelf moving the books to look behind. The night cold fell. Methodically she worked her way down. Her fingers were going dead with the cold.

On the bottom shelf the silver necklace lay a near perfect circle over the jumble of old beads, laces, brooches, make-up, which she kept in a red plastic tray: blob ear-rings, broken watches, a fractured pearl necklace, snapped bracelets, all covered with a silt of dust from many years. The whole shelf was occupied by things she never touched, books she would never read again, scraps of fabric from clothes she had made and thrown away long ago, a browned paper with dead news. All were soft with the fall of dust, except the torn rag which had been laid across the tray, except the shining silver. Its laying out was careful. She did not touch it. If it lay as it was, perhaps it would tell. She sat with it an hour, trying and waiting for the memory of picking it up, handling it, thinking this is the silver chain I gave to Aagot, placing it carefully so. It must have been put there by hand, it must be her own; but no, no. She would not have put it there, there had been no fit of misery to the point of madness, amnesia, in which she would have put it among the memorabilia or junk. It was her bond, uneasy but accepted by Aagot, too heavy and graceless, it would outlast them both. The small winter flowers which Aagot had given her, which lived and then died as she looked after them, outweighed in all values the metal coil she stared at. No memory came to rescue. She invented a jerky and broken film of stopping: staring at the chain on the floor: stooping: holding it up: draping it over the tray: shaking out a rag: draping the rag over: stepping back: forgetting. After a few re-runs it had credibility, the credibility of art, until it came to: forgetting. The screen darkened and flecked. She could not remember or create forgetting. Nothing came to fill the empty space. It was already occupied by a notion which made her feel sick enough to go and vomit.

*

They walked to the street market on a Saturday morning. Hecka had a craving for fruit and vegetables and Aagot thought they should get some exercise.

'I found it,' Hecka said.

'Good. I told you you must have put it somewhere.'

*

'Aren't you going to ask me where it was?'

'Where was it?'

'Under the pillow.'

*

'But I didn't take it off in bed.'

'Where did you take it off?'

*

' . . . No, it wasn't . . . it wasn't under the pillow,' Hecka said.

'Where then?'

'In the kitchen.'

*

'What are you playing at? How could it be in the kitchen?'

'Why not? You'd expect me to find things in an extreme way, if I find them at all.'

'I don't believe you.'

'Why?'

'Because you're lying again.'

*

'Aren't you curious to know the truth?'

'Curiosity killed the cat.'

*

'I cracked an egg and the chain fell out into the bowl with the yolk and the white.'

*

'Tell the truth.'
'You know how dangerous that is.'
'Nonsense.'
'It shames the devil.'
'I'm not interested any more. I don't care where you found it. You've got it, and it's your fault.'
'It's my fault I've got it?'

*

'Why don't you believe it was where I said?' Hecka asked.
'Leave it. Leave it be. There are more important things than a little silver chain.'
'No. Tomorrow and tomorrow the workers lose their chains. Now there is this. Why don't you believe me?'
'I didn't take it off in bed, so that's impossible. Chains don't come out of eggs, so that's impossible.'
'Are they the same kind of impossible? What is possible then?' Hecka asked.
'Lots of things, but not everything.'

*

'Is it possible I found it somewhere else in the bedroom?'
'Yes. That's very possible.'
'Possible enough to be probable?'
'Yes.'
'Probable enough to be true?'
'Yes.'
'Under the carpet, where the corner is scuffed.'
'It's possible, yes.'
'Inside the magazine on the table by the bed?'
'Yes possibly. Shut up.'
'On the window sill behind the curtains?'
'Yes. Yes.'
'On a red plastic tray of beads, under a yellow cloth, on the bottom shelf of the bookshelf?'

'So that's where it was, that's where you put it.'

*

'Possibly, probably, or for sure?'
'You must have done. You know you forget things.'
'So you always tell me. But only the future. Not the past.'
'How can you remember the future?'
'I'm beginning to.'

*

Hecka opened her purse and took out the chain. It swung from her fingers.
'Here you are.'
'I don't think I want it.'
Hecka knew. It hurt just as much.
'Why?'
'You've spoiled it.' Aagot was deeply upset . . . 'First you lose it . . .'
'You lost it, I didn't.'
'No. I mislaid it, you lost it. Then instead of giving it to me and saying where you'd put it, I get all this stuff. I really don't want it any more. You've spoilt it.'
'Aagot. I can't stand this. I'm not strong enough. Tell me the truth.'
'*You* ask *me* . . .'
'No. All right. Act it then . . .'
Aagot's face was distorted by rage, fear, incomprehension: Hecka couldn't read it.
' . . . You acted it before, when I was in the kitchen. Go on. Act. Act: "I don't think I want it any more". Save me Aagot. Save me. Show me how you do it so I can go on loving you without dying of it. I can't live without you. Do this for me. Show me: "I don't think I want it any more".'
They were walking then by the outskirts of the market, passing the first stalls and open shops. Hecka was dragging and trailing, her voice to Aagot's back. Aagot turned her head briefly sideways and said
'Be quiet. People will think you are mad.'
'Is it like this?'

144

Hecka ran, Aagot gripped her arm and jerked her to halt. Hecka's shoulder bag fell onto the road.

'Stop it,' said Aagot 'See what you've done now.'

Hecka pulled away and felt her sleeve tear. An old furniture shop had pieces out on the pavement.

'Was it like this? Is this how it is done?'

She gestured dismissal from a room with three flips of her hand, stood with her head on one side listening, smiled a crooked smile, crept to the tables, chairs, chests, ran her hand over wooden backs and sides, stopped to listen, scraped a wooden chair heavily across the paving, wrenched open drawers and pushed them hard shut, swung the necklace from her finger in pretence of thought dawning, crept hunched to the kerb where there was a plastic rubbish bin already topped with rinds, broken wood, empty take-away food boxes, uneatable fruit, a broken toy, unwanted stuff, and slowly coiled the silver ring over the top. She stood back, stuck for the last piece. The shopkeeper came out.

'Anything you're interested in?'

'Yes, a cloth, a small one.'

'Got some chair backs. Antimacassar. Nice hand work. Victorian.'

'Old? I'll have one.'

'They're inside. Come and choose.'

'Any one. The top one. Whatever comes to hand. I haven't much time.'

Aagot was watching white and still from the middle of the road. Hecka's bag lay at her feet spilling tissues and combs.

'You're a lunatic. An ape.'

She wore her badges of coming out, which Hecka had always admired, the courage. Hecka had settled for reserve and peace, finding it difficult enough to move through agora, hoping not to be noticed, phobic to an extreme. Now Aagot demanded an end to this public display.

'You should be locked up. Gagged. Stop it before people notice.'

Hecka was fading anyway. She fetched a tissue from her bag and laid it over the necklace, no longer possessed. Aagot picked up the bag, put it on Hecka's shoulder, and pushed her forwards quickly before the shopkeeper came out.

*

Hecka opened the mouth of her old shopping bag.

'You know it's perfect nonsense,' Aagot said.

'Perfect.'

Hecka cried street tears. Not a muscle of her face moved. Her eyes dazzled with the oranges and reds of fruits. They filmed and then flooded politely.

'So why do you make up such things? Why tell such lies?'

'No reason. Six oranges please.'

'Six is too many.'

A smear of orange liquid cascaded into the bag.

'One of them is bad,' Aagot said.

'Never mind. Leave it be.'

'But it's bad.'

'Yes. And potatoes please. Three pounds.'

'Reds or whites?'

'Reds. Reds.'

'Whites are cheaper, can't you see?' said Aagot.

'No, not very well. I'm sorry.'

'What for, though? Probably the wrong thing.'

'Everything. Even if you'd done it, it was evil to think of you doing it.'

'That's not good enough. I didn't do it. Do you believe me?'

'Yes. No. Tomatoes.'

'Which?'

'Those.'

'Pound?'

'Please.'

Aagot spoke through Hecka and the stall holder . . . 'I don't know how you think of these things. Nobody else would. People don't do things like that. Those tomatoes are better than those.'

'But you wouldn't take the present back from me again.'

'And so you make up this story out of nothing. No woman in her right mind would want it back after what you'd done.'

146

'That's it,' said Hecka. 'I've forgotten what I done. Did. It's so far back.'

'There's a lot of people waiting here. There's a queue,' the fruitseller said.

'Sorry. How much?'

Hecka paid. He looked at her drenched face.

'Lover's tiff?'

'Yes.'

Oddly he said nothing ugly.

'It's all part of the game.'

'Come on,' said Aagot, fearing the start of a new episode.

'I never was any good at games,' Hecka said.

'Ah. Great handicap that,' the man said. 'Have to learn to be a good loser. There's art in that.'

'Yes.'

*

'Come on. Why did you talk to him? Are you crying?'

*   *   *

'I think I should have a lover,' says Aagot.

Hecka, caught on an in-breath, cannot breathe out.

'A lover?'

'Yes. I think I should.'

'What am I then?'

'I mean, another lover. I never meant to be monogamous.'

'You didn't say another lover. You said a lover.'

'But you know what I mean.'

'I think you mean what you say.'

No answer.

'You pusillanimous little cow. What's "should" about it? And what's monogamy got to do with it?'

'Well, when I say I want a lover, perhaps that's not quite it.'

The silence with its charge of cruelty and pain could go on for ever. For Hecka it is infinite, in that it is changing all the past, everything that has happened didn't happen, she mis-read the whole text, the present is out of all control with pain and

147

confusion, the future she foresees as severed and impossible for her to live in. It is her own fault for failing to remember. For Aagot, what: it seems she has made a complete statement, it appears from her calm face and no-change to be level, the same as fifteen minutes before when they were talking about the best way to break cold white paint. The old unequal battle has to be fought again. Hecka knows her words fall through the air, dead dust to scuff at Aagot's feet.

'I'm not your lover then?'

'I didn't say that.'

'You did. You said you wanted, I mean should have, a lover.'

'I told you, that was a mistake.'

'Why? Why do you want another lover?'

'I told you, I never meant to be monogamous.'

'I don't understand. It sounds like some big word for a terrible thing you want to do. To me.'

'You take everything so personally. It's my life.'

Hecka is walking clumsily around the room.

'But it's me. It's me you're rejecting. Can't you understand how much you hurt me?'

'I can't see why. I'm not rejecting you. I'm just saying it's not enough.'

'Jesus.'

Hecka is having trouble breathing.

'What is "it"? What "it" is not enough.'

Aagot doesn't refute the item. Instead she says with irritation, 'I think I need more freedom now. I feel able. Stronger than I was.'

'Good for you. God help anyone who's near you when you're really strong.'

Aagot says 'That's not fair. Can't you understand?'

'Not,' says Hecka, 'unless you tell me.'

There is silence again. Aagot is visibly oppressed. It enrages Hecka.

'Can't you see that you hurt me?'

'You often hurt me,' says Aagot.

'Can we talk about this one now? This is the one, now.'

A late autumn wasp has blundered in through the window. It

148

settles on the leaf of a plant on the sill. Hecka, blundering too in the sudden change of season, picks the leaf and encourages the wasp onto her wrist, on to the soft veined underside. She watches the wasp flex its abdomen and her upper lip sweats expecting the sharp pain. Aagot ignores this folly. Hecka stands where she must see. Oddly, her act catches one of those forgotten tracks, mossed over, a short cut back which carries you guided past all the lanes and crossings you have turned into, you recognise them all as a story remembered, for a fraction you see each and everything, but never reach the beginning. It is sudden, unbeckoned, impossible to keep or describe. Wherever the path begins, it seems farther back than any chronology as 'born in' would begin. It is not deja vu. It is not opening or closing of the synapses. It is the true and untellable story. And she wonders why it happens now, in this crisis when she is stupid and cannot walk this present short track without blundering and falling. She says nothing of it to Aagot.

'Are you telling me you already have another lover?'

'No.'

'Do you mean you have someone in mind?'

'No.'

'Then it's even more to do with me.'

'Why?'

'If someone lovely had come your way I could understand my bad luck. But if there's no one then it must be my defects that's done it.'

Silence.

'Please help me.'

'I'm sorry. I didn't mean to hurt you.'

'Really? That's nice of you. Thanks for not meaning to. See this wasp.'

'Yes.'

'If it stings it will hurt like hell.'

'Well, you put it there.'

Hecka is caught in her own gesture. The wasp cannot be dropped like a razor.

'And if I say you did you'll say I'm mad. Could you volunteer a little more information.'

'It's difficult. You make it difficult. Anyway, you've had another lover since you've known me.'

'I haven't. I went to bed once with a friend months ago. Is that what you mean by having a lover?'

She is hopeful for a moment.

'No, not quite.'

'Tell me what quite you do mean.'

'You make it so difficult.'

'I expect so. But still, please.'

'If only you weren't so extreme.'

'I am in extremis.'

Aagot is stone still. Hecka looks at her and sees only the stillness. Aagot shows nothing else. She does not even look up. The wasp throbs slowly. One such torment is enough. Hecka pulls a leaf and occupies herself in persuading the wasp to walk off. At the same time she asks Aagot

'Please explain. Please.'

'There's nothing to explain.'

'To yourself, maybe. To me, there is.'

'Can't you understand? I want freedom.'

The wasp has its front paws on the leaf. The dangerous end is bobbing over the vein in her wrist.

'Freedom . . . oh god it's going to sting me before it goes.'

'Why do you do such silly things?'

*　　　　　*　　　　　*

It emerged, it cannot be said that it was said, that there was someone else whom Aagot hoped to make her lover. Hecka, slow-witted, at last reminded her that she had said there was no one: Aagot answered that there was no one who was her lover and that the prospect of this love was not crucial to her desire for another lover. No, she did not say desire, she said search. She needed freedom and not monogamy. She stopped all talk with this unassailable statement. Hecka could only understand it from her own life, a faulty measure. She had been promiscuous, had two or more bed-mates and enjoyed it, but knew it was different in kind from loving Aagot. It was sexual, social, a relatively coarse grabbing at experience.

150

Loving Aagot was erotic and exclusive because it contained everything she wanted. She was possessed. Aagot was not.

Their paces as they walked along the canal path brought them into collision and jumble until Hecka gave the choice of foot-land over to Aagot and walked herself over the ruts, stones, and coarse grass. They did not counterpoint spurts and hesitations. Hecka understood it was no use to try and impress her pain on Aagot or expect to see marks of guilt or even recognition. You would as soon expect the rock you gash yourself on to be torn by your impact and cry out or be aware of its part in hurting you. It is a stone: it is your problem if you fall onto it.

Hecka resorted to abuse, trickery and attempts at minor violence. For her, they were stoical, next best gains to wild confessional which was what she craved to be given and gave herself to excess. If two perform this, there is a sacrament present, if one does it alone there is madness. These games of abuse and trickery were laments and rages. They put a grin on an ugly face and gave cushion blows. They were the larks of a dummling who hopes to melt the princess and win her with silliness. She won amusement and tolerance. At least the performance did not turn Aagot back to stone.

They walked on the tow-path. Hecka prattled. There was a small chance that humour and tolerance, which is to say relative indifference, might pose and hold over some of the time soon coming when she would be alone and liable to extremes, incompatible accounts: this must be the painful heart of the matter, but it could not be so because another story was true. The poles were more to do with who was wicked and who was not, than with limpid understanding. How could I? How could she? At such times she wished for Aagot's perception of truth staring you in the face. Aagot did seem to arrive without travel or travail at clear destinations where she could put down her light baggage and say this is where it is. I am sure. Hecka's frenetic rushes at and retreats from dead ends in the maze, carrying this back-pack and abandoning it for another, got her nowhere near the heart of the matter.

Hecka filled her heart with her own talk that afternoon.

She indulged herself, for once not at Aagot's expense. Sweetness, this rare time, was a possibility of her nature. By the time they were eating cake and drinking tea in the summerhouse of the park she had reached casual melancholy, vague nostalgia, a nice ending to a short story. She talked like an old woman who meets a love of her youth by chance and they smile with autumnal wisdom and kind feelings. Aagot appeared to be playing the same bittersweet etc.

To script this final scene she had improved on nature, her own anyway. She threatened Aagot, without menace, that she would come on the bus and spray-paint 'Aagot is a slut + a ore' on her front door. Aagot smiled affectionately. A conversation like this is silly, which is its value. Hecka called her a slag, a little tart, and wished on her and her new lover frigidity, contagious herpes, and discovery by employers. Aagot grinned. Hecka threatened postcards advertising her services in local shop windows, and advertisement in *Time Out*, 'Young girl seeks Macho Male, age immaterial, for fun and games.'

'Will you really?'

'Stop grinning.'

Hecka told her she was a half-wit to give up such a wonderful, brilliant, passionate lover as herself. Aagot said happily: 'I know.' Hecka slowed to walk behind her and pick up a whippy fallen branch to lash her with it. Aagot stepped aside and the branch snapped against a railing. They sat on the grass: when Aagot squatted to stand Hecka shoved her over onto the gravel path with her foot. From the top of a hill Hecka raced her down and won. At the end of this sweet day they played rough tennis, Halt Hill and Young Love versus The East End and the Bad Old Days. The Bad Old Days Won. They won everything.

But Hecka went home alone, and the remission was over.

*   *   *

The end of an affaire, propounded Hecka pompously, is marked by a great release of dismal energy. The insides of forks are cleaned, bills paid, clothes mended, forgotten friends phoned. Putting on your shoes becomes evidence that you can still walk. There is nothing to see, no result, unless you have your eye in for absences of muck.

Speak for yourself, said Aagot.

*   *   *

6. *The Edge*

. . . the whole scene was inferior, and suggested that
the countryside was too vast to admit of excellence.
In vain did each item in it call out 'come, come'.
There was not enough god to go round.

E.M. Forster

'I think you should meet May,' Aagot said.

'Why, what's in it for you, bugsy?' Hecka asked. She chewed nuts offensively.

'There's nothing in it for me. I just think you should.'

'D'you want a nut?'

'No, you know I don't like them.'

'I think you should. They're good for you.'

'Why should I eat things I don't like? You don't.'

'No. Do you mean you want me to meet her?'

'I wouldn't say that.'

'I know you wouldn't say it. Which ones do you not like most?'

'Walnuts. They crack up in bits. They're disgusting.'
Hecka searched in the string bag for the biggest walnut and cracked it carefully along the rim. Even so it came out in five pieces. She offered it, then chewed it with her mouth open.

'Where should we meet?' she asked.

'I thought we could have a drink together.'

'Oh, the three of us, you mean?'

'Yes. Well?'

'I'm trying to see it. There's the three of us sitting at a corner table in the saloon bar of The Red Lion trying not to look like dykes but a hen-party. You sit there looking at both of us and leaving us to speak but we can't say much because of you and we exchange pleasantries, only something more than pleasantries are being handed over, I mime resignation and May and you accept my resignation and it is quite sad and very civilised, really, it's like a happy ending. Only you can't put those two words next to each other. You get the shaming of the true.'

'I get what?'

'The taming of the shrew. The impossible happy ending.'
Nutshell scattered.

'You've got no right to ask such a cosy fraud, such a sacrifice,' Hecka said.

'What have rights got to do with it?'

'I should do it but rights don't come into it? Anyway, it's indecent.'

'I'm only suggesting we have a drink together.'

157

'No, you're not.'
Aagot got up to go.
'You're telling me what I'm doing again.'
Hecka pushed her back into the chair.
'Yes I am. There's nothing mere or only in the all the jumbled world. Try "I only pushed you back into the chair" for size. Does it fit?'
Hecka stood by the door, prepared to fight off exit. Aagot relaxed and became equivalently more beautiful, the choice of action taken from her. She smiled.
'You've no right to stop me from going.'
'None at all. I don't want you to go.'
The phone rang.
'You'd better answer it,' Aagot said.
'It can't be more important than standing here doing what I'm doing.'
'What are you doing?'
'Looking.'
'What do you see?'
Hecka told her. The phone stopped ringing.
Hecka said, 'You don't expect me to take that vision to a pub and hand it over with a round of drinks? It's not currency.'
'And I'm not your vision.'
'No. But I won't abdicate it until I die, and I won't die until I'm ready to.'
'So there?'
'So there.'
'Who do you think was phoning?' Aagot asked.
'Probably Lauren Bacall. She keeps pestering me for a date.'
'Who's Lauren Bacall?'
'Oh God.' Hecka slid to a sprawl on the floor, leaning against the door ... 'Pass me a cigarette. Where have you gone, Slim?'
'You're talking to yourself again.'
'Yes. Just open the door if you really want to go. I'll crumble up like an old mummy if you give me a shove.'
'There's a sweetness about you,' Aagot said, 'in spite of everything.'

158

'So love me, in spite of everything.'
'I do.'

*

The phone rang again after Aagot had left. It was May
suggesting a meeting. Hearing May's drawl for the first time
Hecka asked, 'Are you antipodean?

'No. Just tired. I rang earlier.'

'I know. I was too happy to answer.'

*   *   *

Hecka met May. They sat at a corner table in the cafe. Hecka
looked in at the staff door and the service hatch, May outwards over the tables to the window screened by scented
geranium. Silver sun sparked between the leaves from the
metal of cars passing. There were flashes of silver on May's
face. They did not seem to trouble her eyes. Hecka was
shaded. She found May easy to look at.

'I'm glad to meet you,' Hecka said formally, and with
intent, 'I'd rather meet you than not. And I'm happier to see
you without Aagot. I hope you understand.'

'I'm relieved you changed your mind,' May said.

'Changed my mind?'

'You did want us all three to meet, didn't you? That's the
impression I got. I hope you don't mind, but I wouldn't have
felt easy about that.'

'I refused to meet you with Aagot. That was her idea, not
mine.'

'Peculiar. When she spoke about it I got a clear notion . . .'

'What did she say I said?'

'I really can't remember her making a definite statement
that that was what you wanted, but the impression; I thought
she preferred it this way and you didn't, you weren't keen to
meet me alone.' It was no longer easy to look straight at May.

'This is not a good start. The lights will begin to flicker and
dim in a moment. She has arranged that you doubt me. I'm
not sure how I can stay now.'

'So you think we're being got at, that she's set us up?

Surely she wouldn't ever think of such a devious thing. No, it must be that I misunderstood her.'

'The timing makes this whole thing impossible, unless plans were made long before... No, I'm definitely not thinking it. I refuse to put one foot on that path. I've been there before.' Her refusal meant nothing. She already was where she had been put. She couldn't look at May. Neither of them was speaking. She touched the dusty plastic flowers, marguerites perhaps, in the middle of the table.

'Nice aren't they,' May said. 'I wonder what they dispense if you squeeze them.'

Hecka turned frightened eyes to her. May smiled and tapped the red plastic tomato with sauce in it.

'I've always liked plastic flowers,' May said. 'I look out for new kinds. They do lilac now. That's beautiful.'

Hecka's mind's eye saw the prisoner returning from work in the fields to his cell, heavy droops of lilac hanging from his straw hat, so raised up he can sport flowers and no one will think the less.

'You don't think they're nasty compared with the real thing?'

'The real thing?' May said, she seemed puzzled. 'Oh, a clumsy imitation of flowering flowers, you mean? No, they're like lockets of hair and photos of children, their own place, not in the world of the living nor the dead. They bring to mind all the things you can't keep but have to lose. They bring them to mind, where they should be.'

'Some people prefer them to real ones.'

'Some people suffer loss more sharply than others.'

Hecka was out of her depth with this woman. She heard herself prattling to ward off the silence which held the whole lost encounter.

'I like your name. I like flower names for women. Rose , Lily, May, Poppy. My friend is called Lily. If I had a daughter I'd call her Poppy.'

'The flower for remembering dead warriors.'

But May was smiling. Her face and voice didn't fit her words. Hecka began to see that this was her nature. She realised also how much of her talk with women in recent times had been contentious and biting; how she expected to fight and be mocked, and that May was not doing that. She was not an enemy, not yet anyway. She was lolling and easy, her detatchment slightly affronting, but not disposed to treat Hecka as an enemy, not yet anyway.

'I'm hungry,' May said. 'Do you know this cafe? What should I ask for to get the most on my plate? What are you having?'

'Not much. I'm too greedy to eat a lot.'

'Mm?'

'I binge or starve. I'm not good at balance. Have something with chips. They give you a lot and they cook them twice so they're soaked in fat, polysaturated. Very satisfying. If you like nuts and wholefood I've brought you to the wrong place.'

'I like all food, as long as there's plenty of it. I'm not greedy.'

Hecka was so dismal there was nothing for it but to maunder or moan. Better to maunder to May and moan when she was on her own.

' . . . I've always been greedy. I'd sooner take nothing than take less than the lot. I used to covet whole gardens. I had a small square and a packet of seeds, but that wasn't enough. I wanted Versailles, a knot garden, orchards, Kew, with bunches to pick of all the big ones like delphiniums and peonies and the big daisies. I used to collect jigsaw puzzles of gardens. I didn't like them if there were people or houses in the picture. It had to be just for me, the whole garden. It was like an appetite.'

May laughed. 'You didn't want a posy or an allotment?'

'No, a flaming great bunch of everything. I was taught moderation. Eating was encouraged and frowned on at home. So I ate lots in little bits. "I'd never punish a child through its stomach" I remember my mother saying that. But that's exactly what happened. I could always go to the larder and eat the cold potatoes an hour after dinner. But it was always noticed.'

'You wanted a feast?'

'Yes, not button holes or snacks. Just for me. None of that

161

moderation or sharing. I was taught to take the cake nearest to me on the plate, the flat sponge drop, not to reach across for the one on the other side which was dripping with jam and pink icing. So I waited till after tea and cleaned up whatever was left and they called me the Dustbin. But I had no right to open someone's garden gate and take what I wanted. That was theft, a quite different category of sin.'

'One which takes courage and affront, not one you are invited to fall into?'

'Yes. Just that.'

May was too good a listener. Hecka was overly excited and chattered '. . . and courage from the accusers too. They'd have to stand up and name their objection to me.'

'. . . instead of leading you into temptation and then pretending they had nothing to do with it.'

'Yes. There are some little girls in my street who came and picked the wallflowers in my front garden last year, so I went out and gave them a bunch and told them to come and ask me another time, not just come and take. I thought I'd spoiled it for them and the flowers would be very dull things now I'd put them in their hands: That's how it would have worked for me. But they keep coming to the door and asking for flowers even when there aren't any. I show them the empty ground in November, or the dead plants, but they don't see. I say "come back in May" and they say "can we have some now". They just don't listen when I explain. They don't see the empty ground.'

'So you haven't spoiled their desire. They still believe if they want something enough you'll come up with it, it's there, only hidden. You've appointed yourself maker of flowers. A magical thing to be.'

'But a nuisance for me. And in the end if I can't come up with it they'll hate me and take revenge and pull up the plants and trample things.'

'Flora deflowered? They may just get sad and indifferent and stop wanting things so much.'

'No it just goes underground. I'm still as greedy and demanding as I was, I've learned not to feel it, but I still revenge if I don't get the things I badly want.'

162

'Do they become dull things if you hold them in your hands?'

'It doesn't happen much. My hands kill them if I get them. Mostly I keep knocking at the door asking, then uprooting and trampling.'

'She can't help it, you know.'

'I know ... Anyway, one day I was standing outside a garden gate and a woman came out and said how lovely her garden was and she put on gloves and fetched secateurs and cut me a bunch of the best ones. If you wait long enough ...'

'And stand in the right places. When my father died I went into the garden at dawn on the day of his funeral and picked the freshest of the flowers and put them on his coffin in the crematorium while I talked to him. Afterwards they put the wreaths outside the chapel, but they threw my bunch of flowers away.'

'You talk to the dead?'

'Of course.'

Hecka relaxed and drank her coffee.

'Perhaps you were in the right place. Perhaps they burned your flowers with him.'

'I never thought of that. Perhaps they did.'

Neither of them found it necessary to cringe with nervous laughter, because neither felt stupid nor judged. There was an easy pause, and Hecka said, 'Your name is a death flower too, like poppy and violet.'

'May? Is it?'

'Yes. When I was little we moved out of London to the country and I picked masses of flowers, cowparsley and dandelion, and my mother put them in jam jars until she said "no more". I picked some sprays of may blossom. They were difficult to get at and I thought they were rare, that off-pink with brown specks and dry smell, I took them to give to the Browns who lived opposite us. They were like uncles and aunties to me. I must have wanted to please them I suppose, or I'd used the last jam jar at home. When I took my present into their house they didn't say anything and I left it on the kitchen table. I didn't understand why they didn't speak, but all adults puzzled me, their silences and their words so I

163

wasn't surprised. Mr. Brown was ill, I didn't know what the matter was, or if it was serious. No one ever told me important things like that. Within a week of me bringing the may blossom into the house he died. Then I overheard my mother and one of my aunties saying it was me bringing the may blossom into the house that did it. May blossom in the house means a death.'

'I've never heard of that,' said May, 'May for the dead.'

'Maybe it's dead now,' said Hecka.

'How mean of them not to tell you and let you take the flowers away.'

'I think so too. Of course, a girl of any spirit would have cottoned on and left selected death sprigs here and there, but I wasn't a girl of any spirit at all.'

'I doubt that, Hecka.'

Hecka blushed. They were the nicest unfounded words anyone had said to her for a long time, and hardly anyone used her name. May smiled. The silence was easily given and taken. The disturbance was further in. Hecka was speaking to a woman who must be, under guidance, far from sure that her company was welcome, but had still initiated the meeting. Hecka was heavily in debt for the gesture, in the circumstances. She did not know how to discharge the debt, the circumstances were not part of her, but a warp, a discolouring, a change of tone; Aagot had consented to her own absence but was there. Hecka couldn't explain and go, because that would confirm the 'fact' that she did not want to see May alone. She had neither courage nor skill to break the grid. She was miserable. Anything she said would be loss, depletion. It didn't matter what she said. She was so depressed she forgot May was really there and might transcend any doubts of her own or not even care about them. She did not know May.

'I'm glad to know about my name. It fits.' May said.

'How?'

Their food arrived and May took salt and tomato sauce while she thought. Hecka was going through a time of no appetite and had only ordered food to be companionable. She drank coffee.

'How? Well, you were an innocent, but accused . . .' May said.

'No, no I wasn't, but still . . .'

'It's difficult. There are things I hesitate to say.'

'How does your name fit you?'

'That word for a start. I'm epileptic, did Aagot tell you?'

'No, she never told me much.'

'I don't make a career out of it, more of an occasional fling. I had to tell them in the group because I'm breaking through the treatment and can't get stabilised, so I'm likely to fall about. Didn't want to frighten them if something happened on a meeting night. That's it: frightening them.'

'How did they take it when you told them?'

'Hard to say. Anyway, you know there's an unspoken vow of secrecy about what happens in groups. In ours the vow of secrecy binds us from knowing what happens in the group time too. It's mysterious, I don't know how it comes about. Still, they took it variously I suppose. They talked about people they'd known who had fits. Let me tell you, nothing is more annoying than deflection into cousins who've got the same. It's like someone near you dying and everyone asks if the funeral went well to shut you up.'

Hecka picked up a chip to dip in tomato sauce and eat.

'The funeral isn't going too well' she said. May grinned.

'So you don't think you were an innocent then?' May said.

'As a child? No. I think I was meant to overhear and understand that what I did killed an old man. I remember so many whispers of that kind. I learned more from whispers about blood sex sin and death than from any of the precise statements they made to me. I knew more from wordless voices rising and falling behind closed doors, not for my ears. What they told me outright seemed like lies they wanted to believe and telling a child would make them true. They needed me to believe them.'

'Yes. And they are children trying to suppress the whispers they heard.'

'They?'

'We.'

Hecka: 'I was told so several times what I was. It's a fact I

165

was shocked because I didn't know what I was, but that doesn't make me innocent. You don't have to act wilfully to act wickedly.'

'That wouldn't stand up in a court of law,' said May, 'as an idea it's a few millennia out of date.'

'Then so am I. Tell me about your name.'

'Well, I wouldn't have been surprised to find it associated with summoning death. I knew I was a partner, I mean: held hands willingly, and looked at things other children hid and closed their eyes from.'

'You didn't pull the sheet over your head when things rustled in the night? You weren't frightened?'

'Yes, I was. But I like to hold still and let things come close and shatter against me. I held still but I listened and kept my eyes wide open.'

'Your name?'

'Wait. There was a back room in our house which was used to store furniture, Victorian stuff my parents started their married life with and had replaced. Mahogany sideboards and overmantels and brown stuffed chairs. No one went in there. It was dark and completely still. The curtains were brown lace and the windows were always shut. The air was thick to breathe. I knew that room. My mother and sisters avoided it without saying. It was full of evil and I was excited because I had to walk past it along the passage to the bathroom on the back of the house. There was only a dim light in the passage from the glass panel over the front door. When I sat in the bath I was a long way from the living room and the kitchen where my mother and sisters were. They used to take a transistor in there with them when they had baths. I didn't. I let it go quiet. I knew if something chose to open the door of that back room and come to me it would reach me alone and before I could get help.'

May looked up at Hecka for a moment. She didn't blink, didn't seem to see her, or saw her and more, the pupil was too wide and dark.

'Weren't you frightened? Didn't you tell your mother?'

'Yes. No, I didn't tell her. I was frightened. I gained power from being frightened. Because I knew I was more powerful than anything which was out there. It was like a game of Murder. I could kill anything by looking at it and blinking and I could choose when. I could force it back to its closed room. I understood wickedness and was stronger than the hand crawling across the floor, the blood from the tap, the grinning face above you when you look up in an empty room, the dead face behind mine in the mirror, all of them. It filled me with delight. And when I walked back along the passage past the room we understood each other.'

'Were you epileptic then?'

'Yes, I was. You mean, did that give me a mysticism, a kind of gifted insanity? No. What it meant was that I experienced my own dissolution in the moment I went under, not in images of terror, I can't describe the state to you and it doesn't happen now. But I was invaded by something which came from outside me and began to dismember me: no, pull the nerves out of my body, the threads which held me together, so I was disintegrating. And I learned that I was stronger, that I came back. It was a struggle for my life and it left me exhausted and not able to move for hours, but I came back and whatever it was went away. When I was in the bathroom I had to muster a force to equal the fear. I had to know its nature intimately and use its own manners of attack and more, and it cost me and was nothing to do with fancy. I can't explain it. I would if I could. But evil was my familiar and I knew its ways.'

'You don't sound guilty.'

'I never felt it. I was just familiar with evil.'

May knew this needed to be explained but was lazy and confident that if it mattered it would be understood sooner or later.

'. . .But you were guilty?' she said.

'Yes. No. More I was responsible for what I was, and that's a feeling similar to guilt, but not the same.'

'It all came from that one event?'

'Oh, no, lots of things. I had a baby brother and we were in the yard and he sat down on a piece of glass and cut his leg badly so I picked him up and carried him in and my father grabbed him away and shouted at me "what the hell have you done to him". I know I said "I didn't, I didn't do anything" but he was very angry with me and I worried and cried because I didn't know how I could have done it but if they said I had then I must have. I've wondered since if I was a malicious little girl who had to be watched for spite, but it wasn't so, no, really. My parents complained I lacked spirit, was too docile. I resented my brother but I soaked up the pain, expected it, never revolted. I didn't know the glass was there and I wasn't near my brother when he cut himself; and I thought may was just a wild flower like a daisy.'

'Why did you take the blame so deeply to heart?'

'I know, it sounds silly. But there was more, it grew, and I began to understand. I was the natural one to approach pain and death and so I was tainted by them. Cause and effect didn't have any meaning. They were the same. I'd never seen my grandfather but when he was dying I was sent to see him on behalf of his wife and daughter.'

'They didn't go?'

'No. Just me. When he died I was sent to the funeral. When my aunt had to have a major operation she might not recover from I was the only person in the family she told, not because she cared for me but because I was the one to know such things. Of course. When my Grandmother was ill and dying it was for me to nurse her and for my family to insist there was nothing much wrong with her, I was inventing her illness. She died, so I'd invented the cause of her death. When my father died the family was silent and I arranged his funeral and was ashamed. I talked to him too when he was dead. So I learned you see who I am. I was puzzled but I know I was recognised.'

'You had no doubts?'

'No, only difficulties. My mother tried to abort me for very good reasons and it was before the '67 Act and it was clumsy but it nearly worked. So I'd brushed against death before I was born and it was recognised. I became powerful in a way, without any choice or effort or intelligence on my part. Whenever my brothers fell off bikes or out of trees and broke bones or cut themselves I had to bathe and bandage or take them to hospital and hear them cry. It was my job if you like, my responsibility, and somehow my fault. I used to play at fortune-telling cards, games where you shuffle, split, and shuffle, until you're left with three cards, your special ones, to lay out. I always had the death card to lay out. I stopped playing because I thought it meant I was going to die, but that's not what it meant at all. It was my card.'

Hecka needed sustaining.

'Perhaps your parents were right,' May said.

'What do you mean?'

'Perhaps you were too docile. A natural in the old sense. People need an outcast, someone to carry a sack full of trouble around for them. Even a fair share is too much.'

May took sugar lumps from the bowl. She pushed one across the table.

'One for you and one for me.'

She took three more.

'Two for you and two for me.'

She pushed two of them to Hecka's pile and one to her own, so she did have two. Hecka watched dazed until she began to remember the childhood trick of sharing. May took four lumps.

'Three for you and three for me.'

Hecka had six. May had three.

'Wait a minute . . .' Hecka said.

'It must be fair. You heard me counting and you watched.'

'True. And I don't like sugar.'

'You accepted it though, just the same. They talked you into it from birth. You'll never be exactly a comfortable presence, but a necessary one. Perhaps you were born docile for that, a natural.'

'A natural like an idiot?'

'Yes, but they were always special.'

'This kind of thing isn't talked about.'

'No, it's in the anthropology books, applied to primitive societies.'

'I've never talked about it before, except to myself.' Hecka looked at her plate and was surprised to see she had eaten all her food while they were talking.

'More coffee?' May said.

'Yes. It fits. I was never good. Any good acts were ignored. It puzzled me. I gave presents, not death flowers, and they were received with silence. I was never successful even when I was. I got into university around the time my brother failed his 11-plus and I was told I'd injured him because he felt bad as a result of what I'd done. I wasn't embraced and told I'd done well. I'd done badly.'

'You can't be named as good if you're named as bad. But you hear and see things they deny. That's a kind of good fortune, if it doesn't madden you.'

'But I can do good. I've done some good things.'

'Of course.'

'But I also fail because of it, because of me. As I've done now.'

'Aagot?'

'Yes. I didn't know about love. It came too sudden and too late for me. Being loved. It's not in my nature to be loved.'

'It doesn't have to be in your nature. You're confusing agents, stepping over into Aagot's territory.'

'Still: I don't want to, but have to say to you that I'm incapable of love, only some vileness, and am not of the kind that can be loved; and now I don't want to say any more.'

May wasn't moved aside, and seemed indifferent to the hostility.

'Don't let them tell you who you are until you die and don't insist that I am one of them. You know that. I'm sorry for the absurdity.'

'I'm sorry about my obsessions. I didn't mean this to happen.'

'"You don't have to act wilfully to act wickedly"? I'm free to get up and go. I don't want to. Tell me; how did you get to know her?'

This is easier to make a story of.

'Can't rightly say I did that, get to know her first, like you're supposed to. More she picked me up.'

May grinned.

'Come on. She doesn't. She wouldn't.'

'Oh yes she does. Did. Watch out for her. There's more ways

than missing the last bus home and discussing Virginia Woolf.'

'Hell, I should hope so, in the interest of being understood. But Aagot?'

'Well, how did you get to know her?'

'That's not fair, I asked.'

'I don't have to be fair. I'm an injured party. You're a co-respondent.'

'Do you habitually put people in the dock? How Aagot must have suffered. I met her in the group of course.'

'But how? Meeting of minds?'

'Good god no. I was attracted to her. I was heart-free.'

'Cruising?'

May laughed. 'Nothing so energetic. Or so crude. Aagot was very kind in not mentioning how nasty you can be . . . She was silent and neat. Very highly charged.'

'I want her again,' Hecka said, not looking at May.

'Yes. Well. In your terms, I suppose I wanted to mess her up a bit. Anyway she looked at me. And put her cigarette out in the ash-tray near me instead of the one her side of the table. So I knew.'

'Seductress. She seduced you.'

'All right. If you call that seduction.'

'I certainly do. From her, that's asking you to bed. She picked you up.'

'Nothing so crude. And then I threw a fit at the end of a meeting and fell downstairs.'

'What a brainwave.'

'It was only a small one.' May's humour was unshakeable. 'I just happened to be at the top of the stairs.'

'You fell for her?'

'She offered to put me up for the night. When I came to properly I was in her bed.'

'Were you glad?'

'I was not displeased. But I wouldn't call that being picked up.'

'It was exactly that.'

'And she didn't pick you up either,' May said.

'She did, she did. She kept looking at me and made a mess

with papers and tissues and coffee rings all round her. It was as good as inviting me into the cupboard under the stairs.'

'And you ran in and slammed the door behind you.'

'No. If I knew how to shut the door you wouldn't be inside now and me outside. I was far too inept and scared. She laid herself open again and again but I thought I must be imagining things and I'd get the door shut on my fingers. I'm not used to being asked in. I got so nervous I had to find out, but in my own way, simple, so I could understand. I asked her to come out for a drink with me.'

'Why?'

Hecka shrugged. 'It's public, it's brightly lit, a place where she'd have to be precise again, where conversation is expected. I'd be freer and safer because she'd be less so.'

'She might have withdrawn completely.'

'Then I'd know she'd only been playing.'

'So what did you do?'

'I had two drinks and said I loved her.'

'And you say she picked you up?'

'Yes. I showed proper seriousness. She was toying with me. What I wanted to say was "I fancy you" but I was afraid that was what she'd call sexist and I'd find myself alone in the saloon bar trying to look indifferent over my beer glass. Anyway, it's one thing to be walked out on, and another to be walked out on with moral outrage.'

'There's nothing wrong with fancying someone.'

'OK. But you're supposed to debate socialist feminism and radical feminism first and become sisters. I didn't feel like her sister. Still don't. Love is something else, this kind.'

'Yes, but don't despise the myriad other kinds.'

'I don't. I really don't. I only despise lies and cruelty in the name of sisterhood. I love some women very much, but can't pretend to love them all because they're women. That's as flaccid as men's talk of brotherhood. It becomes something very ugly when it's put to any serious test.'

'And your kind of love doesn't include lies and cruelty?'

'It does. They are the stuff of it.'

'Women have enough experience of cruelty to be going on with, to care for each other.'

172

'It kindles brief fires to warm ourselves by, and gives us passions to act together, for a season, I've done it.'

'The fact that you've done it sometimes doesn't make a case against it.'

'I'm not making a case. I'm crying, or I would if I had the grace.'

'Let's go, eh? Have you got time still?' said May.

'Yes, it's still warm. Let's go over to the gardens.' They paid and walked out across the main street and into the communal gardens squared in by flats. Hecka stopped at a confectioner and bought two bars of swiss chocolate, one for Aagot and one to share with May.

'Does she eat chocolate in bed with you?' she asked May.
'No.'

'I wish I hadn't asked. I still hope it's not true.'

'Do you resent me very much?'

'No. I'm sick with her. I'd like to mark her, which is exactly what I've never done, left my imprint. She's stepped in me like wet concrete and walked on. Let's sit on the sunny side.'

In the dead middle of the square there was an artificial hill like a burial mound. It was likely based on clay and rubble from the old buildings, made into an architect's fancy, a reminder of hill. It was round among the planes and angles of glass walls. The time was mid-evening and the light was very sweet and yellow. May flopped out on the slope, her legs curved, one arm looped away from her body, the other dropped across her stomach, and shut her eyes. She's like a rubber bendy toy, Hecka thought. What gives her the right to be so relaxed? She's very irritating. She must know I'm looking at her while her eyes are shut and she doesn't care. What's she doing with all this?

'The hills and the sky is green and blue sky, the rain poured on the land and the grass.'

May opened her eyes and then shut them.

'What happened then?' she asked.

Hecka understood: what happened after 'I love you' in the pub.

173

'I don't want to tell you.'

She remembered. She had used the words which would get her what she wanted, truth or consequences. She had sat the other side of the round table looking at Aagot as much as she dared but in effect fright-blinded when she looked directly. Being frightened confirmed she wasn't telling a lie but facing a truth. She was always frightened if she wanted something or to know something very much and let it be known. She had looked at Aagot's brown arm and blunt fingers holding the glass. She had wanted to stroke from the shoulder and feel the little knob of bone, hold the nape of her neck and shape with her hand down the throat to the unguarded hollow in her breast bone. She smoked and didn't look up. Her corner sight was acute for the occasion. She could see the silver necklace, the blue braclets, the fawn silky top, and enjoyed herself perilously in imagination handling the silver and slipping the silk across Aagot's breasts. It all lacked spirituality, she knew. It felt fine. Aagot hadn't answered yet. Hecka then volunteered her own dismissal.

'I usually say that after my third drink.'

She waited for one of the standard rejections: . . .I like you a lot but I just don't feel like that about you . . .Why do you need to lay that on me? . . .I'm sorry but I already am in a relationship . . .I'm going with some friends to the Conference on Saturday, why don't you join us? . . .'I haven't had time to get to know you . . .Hecka had golloped her beer clumsily and looked around at the people. She wiped them away. She flicked her cigarette ash and missed the ashtray. At last she had dared to look up at Aagot. She was leaning back against the vinyl, smiling. Hecka thought sod it, she's going to make fun of me. Aagot yawned and showed, thank god, slightly imperfect teeth. The yawn was a performance but Hecka hadn't got her eye in yet for her style and didn't understand.

'I think it's time I should go home.'

Aagot mock stretched. Hecka thought: this has to be one of the nastiest things ever done to me, unique, in a class of its own for cruelty.

'That's it, then,' she said, for the first of many times black

sick with rage. After a long pause: Aagot: 'With you I mean.'
The tone said 'Silly'. For the first of many times Aagot held
back the content of language and gave first an empty form, as
if it were enough, as if by not saying herself, she made Hecka
responsible for the statement.

May's eyes were open. Some children had come to play on
the bit of asphalt wired off for that purpose. Three tyres hung
there for them to swing on, but the children had lost interest
in them long before. A concrete tube for crawling through
had been shied at and blocked up with tin cans and bottles.
Now the children were playing Dare, climbing up the mesh
fence and jumping, climbing higher and jumping wider. May
watched, her arms resting on her knees, hands dangling.

'What happened to hoops and skipping ropes?'

'They got incorporated into the educational system.'
Hecka sounded venomous. 'They'll get their hands on Dare
next and call it competitive spacial experimentation. Most of
them will settle for jumping onto rubber mats and marking in
centimetres and like being told they're doing it properly. But
there'll always be some little bugger who remembers the wire
cutting into hands and being frightened landing on the hard
ground.'

'Don't you like me?' May said. It was possible she sounded
sad. Hecka was ashamed. She had spoilt things. The shouts
of the children were coarse, the sunlight dirty ochre, the
green hill a heap of grassed rubble. She lamented with
neanderthal dumbness. She had not even considered that
May might care how she was received, or might have hoped
for amity. Stupid, stupid, she lost everything so. She was
without respect. Now she considered her appraisal of May's
relaxed body with shame; it was facile, her first resort to
degrade. She painted black and then shouted that there was
nothing light to see. Gentleness was lost on her. She was lost
in it. May was Aagot's lover, her sweet, her intimate,
laughter, her kin, heartsease, forgiveness, her future.

'I'm upset as I should be. I'd better go home.'

When she got home she found the chocolate still in her
pocket. She'd lost her chance to persuade Aagot to think of

her for a few moments while she unwrapped the silver paper. She threw the chocolate bars away, having no use for them.

*   *   *

So Hecka did not find out in her conversation with May how she and Aagot had become lovers, which was what she wanted to know. Her self-absorption and despair precluded it. May liked her and was willing to say what she could, but understood it was impossible to do so. When she lay back on the mound between the flats and closed her eyes it was because Hecka tired and disappointed her.

May's love-making began with courtship. She couldn't begin to tell Hecka this in the face of mockery and talk of pick-ups and seduction. Aagot needed courtship and May enjoyed it. They met in Aagot's house for a formally invited meal. It was understood that they both doubted the group's embargo on one to one contacts out of group control. Aagot cooked and presented a careful meal and they talked about the food, the cat, films, furnishings and holidays.

May's indolence was sweet to Aagot. There was no carping and no fear. They smiled over glasses of wine and sat close for warmth by the fire. There were no probing questions or challenges. Aagot felt the delicacy and the security the more for her long exposure to distress and demands. Nothing was demanded of her, but May was glad to be near her, that was clear. Love-making, as Hecka would have understood it, did not happen. For Aagot and May it did. They kissed gently and laughed. They finished the wine and went to bed together and slept in embrace.

They met frequently and without formal arrangement as their familiarity grew. May took to calling at Aagot's house straight from work once or twice a week, and they went out together at weekends. Love-making was not formalised into expectation that they would decisively take off their clothes in the bedroom and act towards a special kind of fulfilment. Aagot often felt she had been made love to after a cup of coffee, some laughter, words about this or that.

May was aware of absences, blanks when words faded off

176

the page and Aagot demanded silence by reducing language to vacuity.

'Were you in love with your husband when you married him?' (Tell me about you and him.)

'When I married him? At that time, no, I don't think I was.' As if the issue were the exact time of her feelings, not what she had felt.

It happened whenever May mentioned Hecka.

'Have you heard from her recently?' (Tell me about her . . .)

'No, not recently.'

But May had been used to reserve all her life and wasn't given to rages about it.

The seeds of the end of their affaire were, oddly, the reverse of what had finished Aagot and Hecka. May was gentle, respectful and placid. She moved with all this and a fine intelligence among many women friends. Aagot watched her offering the same indolent sweetness all around and began to be distressed that she was not singularly treated. It was not that she wished for the appalling distinction of being Hecka's one and only lover, but some savour, even a bitter one, was missing.

Then May went off at short notice, twice, to spend a week with different friends: Aagot experienced the absence as loss, May did not, and was indifferent to Aagot's upset when she returned. She listened and showed understanding, but it was not enough. Aagot learned that she required more distinct recognition when she loved.

But it was a long and happy affaire in which she recovered as from a powerful infection and she came out of it more acute. Her needs, which she characteristically expressed as more time, more space, but which were in fact a need not to be frightened by pressure and demands, had been met. It was, in the same terms, an afternoon affaire, in the control and consciousness of daytime, not, as with Hecka, a night affaire in which she was ridden by shocks and fright she could not understand or, above all, control.

*   *   *

Hecka had short fits of mindless hope. She thought: how silly the slaps of cruelty, the unfinished business; rather that they are contained safely in love. It spurted out like the desire for food in a fast, a forbidden cigarette. Why not have, what is the value of denial? Thinking on the singleness and limit of her life, or listening to a sloppy romantic song, it was absurd to push down the longing to hear Aagot's voice immediately, to see her face as soon as possible.

Sometimes she succumbed and telephoned. Aagot spoke to her as if she were in an importunate debt-collector, a nuisance. Hecka would ask anything so that she could hear her speak, the delicate precise voice. It was a speeded play of the whole affaire, from hope as she dialled to emptiness in a few minutes. It was always worse after than before. She herself had chilled off lovers in the past. It was a degradation to hang about when the welcome was gone, and to remember when such interruptions were occasions of joy. She forgave herself though, and expected Aagot to put up with it for as long as it would be needed. Aagot didn't put the phone down on her, but made it clear she was busy getting supper, preparing work, or tired. Aagot owed her nothing, but all the same Hecka would try to snatch a little. At such times anything was better than nothing. At other times, when she was calm, that is forgetful, nothing was better.

In the first days of their separation she wrote letters to Aagot. One or two she sent, most she tore up.

'Let me come back': she wrote. Aagot did not reply. It was kinder that she did not. Hecka wrote:

'Aagot, I shan't let you go. I shall drag at your skirts and whine, and put stones in your path so you stumble and I can intercept you on your way, and sting you with nettles, and rage, and cry. Until you let me in. I am elected to be your lover. My body affirms it as I write, in its centre of intelligence and love, it opens and moves toward you. Let me in.'

A week later an envelope came in Aagot's hand. Hecka feared to open it. She carried it to work and opened it at lunchtime in the canteen when its impact would be blunted by noise, company and pre-occupation. Aagot wrote:

'I am sorry that I make you suffer, but you made me suffer

a lot too. It could never have worked. We are too different. I am happy now and wish you were too. I hope you find a more suitable lover. I'm going to the Conference on Saturday with some friends. Why don't you come with us?'

It seemed absurd to her, and checked her from writing again. A more suitable lover? Too different? It was outside the range of her understanding. It was being unsuitable, different, that made love worth enduring. She threw the letter away.

Good friends helped her. She accepted all meetings and initiated others, and listened engrossed to all that was said. Friends gave her much more than in the days long before when she had been calm and different. She did not speak to them much about her state. To some women friends her dykedom was an embarrassment they endured because they cared for her. She did not want to see them struggle to believe that her pain was as valid as theirs would be with men. She feared, with some grounds, that lesbian friends would commiserate, but in terms which would make her feel worse because they might not conceive, or speak, as she did. She did not want to hear the words Relationship or Scene or Get It Together.

Lily broke her. Hecka told her that her love affaire was over. 'Nothing lasts forever.' Lily said.

Hecka said: 'But you said maybe Mrs. Harris and Tom and Vicky and May might all live.'

Lily said: 'Mrs Harris died two weeks ago.'

Hecka cried helplessly.

*   *   *

Hecka tried to settle down. She had no idea how far down was. She told herself many stories accounting for what had happened, in shapely ways, some rich, generous to them both even in judgment: she used the 'I' of a god to speak of she and she, and made a flimsy pinnacle which collapsed into a mess of scraps each time it was completed. She picked up torn fragments of misery, blame, contempt, disgust, and pawed them until they were filthy with handling and picking at their rag edges. All were specious.

179

She worked hard, remembered to eat, made a system of occupation, paid her bills, got her eye in for absences of muck, and kept for some weeks the resolve that whatever her versions, however unbelievable that she had lost and had to go on, one thing was clear: she must leave Aagot untroubled. She was buoyed up in shallows. Desire rested. She practised stoicism more vigorously than ever in her life.

It ended. In the middle of a night she woke because of pain. It shocked so that her eyes opened and she was more violently awake than if a voice had shouted in her ear. The pain was unfamiliar. It came from somewhere in the middle of her body, but not stomach or guts. It spread and hurt strongly up through her throat and mouth and down. She moved carefully to put the green lamp on, carefully to shift and sit up. The pain didn't change with movement. She was badly frightened. The source of the pain couldn't be located, she had no name for it. Perhaps it was one of the organs she'd never had to be aware of: liver, pancreas. She looked at the clock. It was ten minutes past two. It was difficult to breathe. The pain was steady and pitched high, her awakeness terrible. She reached for her bag which always went with her to lie by the bedside, and turned it out to find the specific, the insurance just for this, whatever it was. There was nothing. She was not covered.

It was Aagot. Hecka had gone under and was drowning in her own muck pool. The remission was over. Prisoners keep a condemned man awake all night before his execution to spare him drugged sleep broken at five a.m. by the forcible, substantial, grey ministers of death. She had drugged herself, and now she was forced awake and knew she had lost everything lovely, though love was still there beyond her perception; everything fine, comic, all fights, joy, care, rage, all attributes were gone and she was in a world of flecked grey and would remain there. She had no voice with which to call Aagot: come, to me, come; and no place to call her to.

She grew accustomed to the pain as an invalid does. She was invalid as the many old who wash and dress, shop, walk, exchange the time of day, with no meaning because all meaning is buried, or burned.

Where she had gone wrong was: she should never have told the lie that she fancied making marmalade. That was a more futile and absurd way of accounting for all that had happened, and so more appropriate than most.

*   *   *

Hecka read palms and was modestly superstitious. In a man-made world filling with expanded polystyrene, spreading with tarmac, and levelling with common sense, she kept mostly secret a sense that parts of eco-systems, certain places untouched by human hand, useless although worried over by ecologists because Man is responsible for his environment: they knew her and recognised her. They even accosted her. It was of course borderline insanity and she kept quiet about it.

There had been a week in her life when birds visited. She alone in a London street had two nests of house-martins under her eaves, the birds returning every year to shrill and nag and dive-bomb her as she walked to her front door. They shat precisely and apparently with purpose over the rim of their nest so that she witnessed the fall and plop and the mounting heap of grey and white mess on the window sill. Their presence was assertive and certainly not appealing, nor requested. They made sure she knew they were there.

In that one week she had walked in a wood and a shiny black bird, but not a blackbird, had beckoned her with oddly human, easy to understand jerks of its head, as in 'come this way, come'; a few hops, a pause, another gesture, now and then stopping to dibble the dry leaves with its beak, and Hecka had followed, leaving the path, thinking vaguely of the Brothers Grimm and also of the common explanation that it was a mother bird tricking her away from the site of a nest of babies, but not knowing for sure. Then the bird stopped only a few feet from where she stood, and waited as if it were Hecka's move, but she didn't know what was expected of her so she just stood and the bird appeared to give up on her and flew away. Then she was in a bedroom and in the morning when she rose and pulled the curtains a sparrow was outside threshing its wings with violent energy, not equipped to stand on air as a

181

humming-bird, to stay in her sights, until exhaustion or pain made it drop and perch. Hecka had no idea what it was up to. Then, by this time with some fright, she saw a kestrel clawed on the handle of a mower three feet from her back door. It looked.

Hecka had no feelings for birds. She did not know it was a kestrel until she looked at pictures in a book. There was no doubt. She never fed pigeons in the park, or searched birds' eggs as a child, or thought to climb a tree to investigate a nest. Suddenly they were seeking her out as if they had something to do with her. They pestered her. She mentioned the events to a couple of friends. One explained each incident as in its own way a recognisable piece of bird behaviour, and the fact of the three together as coincidence, and said that things tend to go in threes anyway. The final words seemed to contradict the nature of the rest of the statement. If things tend, that is not coincidence. Hecka was no wiser. Coincidence meant that the events happened together, or near, and she knew that already. The under-meaning of the word was that no meaning could sanely be considered. The other friend, who was interested in the therapeutically mystical, suggested that the dead were trying to get in touch with her through birds. At this point Hecka gave up telling, but continued to move with suspicion. She thought privately: perhaps birds because I never notice them, don't like them; I am accustomed to the smile or sneer implicit in the behaviour of a cabbage or a rose. Rocks and stones impinge on me more.

She read palms mostly as a party trick, or so she presented it. She knew that we all read all flesh. It was just that there seemed to her to be a particular concentration held in the cup of the hand, as there is written plain in the face, as there may be concealed in the womb. There is no cabal in reading a face. Palms were a lark, a slightly risky truth and dare game, a chance to indulge in crazy talk, a quiddity, a jocular permission to pretend; let's pretend for a while that meaning and intention extend beyond the next five minutes, that there might be shape, which we all know cannot be because Man Makes Himself. As He goes along. His steps create the path. His last footfall makes a clearway for other Men. Before Him, chaos and old night until His pocket torch and boots make clear and open. How could it be otherwise since He is the King of evolution? If the path were already cleared, then others would have gone before and He would not be the Maker, moment by His own momentum. The earth laboured, not knowing what She was doing, and from Her will-lessness brought forth will, they say.

As Hecka concentrated on an offered hand the tiny lines, the centimetres of up and down, the shades of near same, bits of soft and hard, warm and cool, became a landscape. Tracks narrow, confused with crossing lanes, broadways as decisive as Roman roads, great rounded hills, chunks of hard rock, landfalls, places where it was warm and restful, places where a sphynx lurked, all scale went, as with a lover all bounds and bonds were broken.

Once, sitting with Lily and talking about what futures they saw for themselves with no crystal ball, Hecka got bored with the prosaic statement she was making; if this occurs, then that, and she leaned across the paper-covered table in Lily's room, held her own hand out, and offered to read Lily's palm. Lily's eyes narrowed and she closed and retracted her hands and said 'Don't mess.' Hecka understood. Lily wasn't withdrawing from touch, that final cruelty, nor was she saying that the idea was silly.

Aagot had seen Hecka perform her trick at a party, looked and listened, but not offered. A few days later when they were alone, she had said 'Read my hand.' Hecka was enchanted. She asked for the left hand as she always did: Aagot had thrust forward the right.

'Why?' said Aagot.

'I don't know,' said Hecka. Aagot looked suspicious, but put out her left hand.

'Open it then.' Hecka said.

'Do I have to?'

'Of course.'

Aagot stretched her hand, fingers splayed wide and arched backwards. The skin was strained and no blood flowed, the centre valley was desert white, the mounds of flesh between the finger bones yellowed. The stubby finger pads mottled purple red with stilled arterial blood.

183

'Relax.' Hecka said.

'How?'

'Let your hand go limp, as if it's doing nothing.'

Aagot turned her hand over, back up, limp on her knees. Hecka saw a tortoise in its place, the finger ends the tortoise feet-stubs under the shell back.

'Turn it over now.'

Aagot turned it over, rigid.

'I can't read it like that.'

'Why? You read two hands at the party.'

Hecka bent Aagot's fingers inwards. They obeyed the pressure but stuck in a claw, rigid. Hecka took her wrist and shook her hand up and down. The wrist moved but the hand held firm as if it were an object held by the wrist, as unbending as a thermometer held and shaken. Hecka looked again, then made a sly grab for Aagot's right hand. Aagot, always quicker witted, put her right hand behind her back and kept her left hand tight.

'I can't,' said Hecka.

'Why not?'

'You've wiped it out. You've made it blank.'

'So it was only a trick at the party. You were just making it up as usual.'

'Of course I was making it up. What else is there to do? But maybe it's there to be made up.'

Hecka's own hand was familiar to her. The life-line held her. It was sliced across, at early middle-age, by a decisive slash which terminated it. She joked and said, that's the 38 bus which is moving at its usual stately pace from the depot to run me down one wet afternoon. That is my 38 bus. I have been waiting for it for a long time. It will catch me in the end.

She had time for only one thought before she was absorbed by the fire of pain, drowning in blood, the pressing of bone or stone: that she'd got it wrong. It was a 253.

A woman on the pavement dropped her shopping bag and tins and tomatoes rolled out. Inside her bag an egg broke slimily. A small crowd stood in the rain but went away soon. There was not much to see. The dead woman was not smashed to a pulp. They had seen better on newsreels, in films. They

184

walked on. Drivers went quickly, to avoid being called as witnesses. The bus stopped of course and the driver got out. The passengers complained. They had already suffered delays. The woman could not be seriously hurt. She was talking still, still talking, though no one could understand what she was saying because the sounds were liquefied. Only a middle-aged woman stood on the pavement, her bag at her feet, weeping, a parody of all silly middle-aged women. A young couple laughed as they walked by.

Hecka was pronounced dead on arrival at the hospital. Odd sounds still came from her throat, no words, a broken chant, long after it was medically agreed that her heart had stopped beating and her brain was dead. A young intern, disturbed by it, pushed a long pad of cotton wool into her mouth. Then it was quiet and commonplace. A nurse called his eyes and attention for a moment. When he turned back to cover the body and be done, he saw the white pad had moved up and out of the woman's mouth, it's centre drenched in blood. He was young and not hardened. He had not witnessed many of the strange actions of death. His fears were three fold; that she was not truly dead; that his childhood stories of the dead refusing to accept their condition, the base of all ghost stories, were true; that the dark red pad was woman. He could not touch it, clear her mouth. He pulled the sheet over her body, swished the utility curtain across the cubicle wishing for heavier drapes, better still a wall, and got busy with a straightforward case of a child with a burnt arm. It was a relief that there was no blood, no mouth, this time.

It was many months later that Aagot learned of Hecka's death. May had known and presumed that Aagot did. By that time May had abandoned all conversation about previous loves with her. The deflection into time, place, the mathematics of psychology, had got her nowhere. She accepted it. She loved Aagot easily, took what was given, and had no need to shout for more.

May came back from one of her weeks away with friends. Aagot felt betrayed by her casual coming and going and she had been lonely. She was angry but could not recognise, express or answer to her state. She had learned, so many years ago, that there are other ways. May failed to recognise it.

Aagot questioned her about the wheres and whens of the holiday. She interjected an occasional connection: she had done that too, been to a place like that. Order prevailed. May was not disturbed by the distance. She knew it would shift when it could shift. She was patient. Aagot was the ruler and marked the distances. The empty space, the cold, was the only way she could tell her anger.

'What have you been doing all week?' May asked.

'Nothing much.'

May was insensitive to the accusation, to her guilt. She lolled, all the time in the world. Aagot picked up her knitting.

'Have you missed me?' May asked.

'I don't know. It's hard to say. I've been busy.'

'Doing nothing much?' She regretted it as she said it. 'Can I embrace you?' she asked.

Aagot sat upright in her chair. She did not say no. It became May's risk move.

'So what did you do on Saturday afternoon?' Aagot asked. She had been following closely, tallying the hours and movements. Saturday afternoon had been unaccounted for.

'Oh yes. We went for a walk.'

'Where to?'

'No special direction. We walked down lanes full of meadowsweet, and talked.'

'What did you talk about?'

Aagot meant: whom did you choose to talk to, and was it different from talking to me.

'I don't know, I remember cats and children and martyrs and wholefood and the virgin Mary and dreams and trousers. I don't know.'

Aagot selected martyrs, Mary, dreams, for their absurdity. She was very angry.

'. . .and how we were frightened of cows, and whether we were scared of death. And I thought of Hecka's funeral.'

'What funeral did she go to?'

May was puzzled.

'Her own of course.'

'How can you go to your own funeral?'

'How can you avoid it?'

Aagot was upset. May was playing with words, as Hecka used to, instead of telling a simple truth. At that moment she had choice, to change the subject or to impress her anger on May. Because the betrayal was made worse by this slippery talk she persisted.

'Who, in fact, had died?'

'Hecka. Aagot, what are you playing at?' The accusation echoed.

'Hecka died?'

'Yes. I thought you knew.'

'When?'

'A few months ago.'

'How?'

'A bus, she was run over. The driver said she didn't seem to know where she was or what she was doing.'

'Where?'

'I don't know.'

'What time of day?'

'I don't know.'

'Was she cremated?'

'I expect so.'

There could be no hesitation.

'Cremation is cheaper. I was nearly run over once. In Rome.'

It was for May as when she had lived through a small earth tremor, everything had lurched for two seconds and then stilled, or when she had seen Fay's face slowly turn. Impossible. Then normal.

'She's dead,' May said because it seemed that Aagot had not understood, had felt no shift.

'Mm. My aunt died last October.'

And so was death shrouded now by a thin curtain, covered with a rag to trick the eye away.

*   *   *

7. Come come

Make an effort to remember. Or failing that, invent.
Monique Wittig.

I wake early every morning and realize with joy, breath let go: this is my place. When I was younger I woke later, reluctant, and my first awareness was: oh god, here is the day again, I am in the same place, I never made it, I have to win it or survive it. There was no joy; I breathed in and held on. Now I wake early and am in it. I don't understand and I don't care to try. If I did I would be back in the days of thinking, picking holes in the slightest ease which came to me. Thinking as I did then always ended with something poked stretched and torn, picked raw. But joy; it can only be so or not.

When I wake I think of the wood splintering at the door frame. I always see the jag of wood. It does not make me think: I should get that mended. I am glad that it splits a little more, slowly, as months go. I inspect it, do not pick at it. When I wake I think of the yellow paint which is flaking away from the wood on the porch. I do not think: I should recover that. I watch its curl and find new places of wood left exposed. I am glad that it flakes a little more, slowly, as the seasons go. This is my place. It accords with me as I age and change. It does not oppose me. I don't have to survive it or win it. It does not drive me daily into unwanted tasks. I do only what I find myself doing. I can only tell the joy by telling what it is not.

It is not the presence of people to love. I have loved and believe in that more perhaps than anything I have now, but it cannot be claimed and kept and I have worn through grief. It is not the presence of affectionate friends, however passing and sweet. I have had that, and I believe in it. It is not the trying for success, competence; I have been successful and competent and I know their value.

All of them are good, excellences. I do not know what has happened that I no longer go looking for them, no longer go looking at all. All I need is my place.

I wake early, I know it is because of the thin clear light. I never pull curtains at night. I like the waking to thin light. The few things in my room are so delicate with it they could lift and dance. Later in the day it thickens. I stretch out and pick up the old cushions from the floor. Their covers are unstitching and dirty, but they will last as long as I will. Everything here will last as long as I will. I will lose nothing, never suffer from losing anything again. I poke them behind me until I lie sleeping as in death-bed pictures, but I do not die yet, I look at the thin light and the new sameness of things. The same things are created every morning, my mugs and two chairs and curtains and cupboard and clothes hanging on nails. Then I pull my bed cover up to my chest, lay my arms on or under it depending on the weather, and give myself waking sleep, the sweetest because the new light enters my closed eyes and between our powers we make stories to remember and examine all day, if I want to, there is no business to stop me, I am learning to remember. Sometimes I do that for a whole day. My bed cover is an old big table cloth, I forget where from. It still has pink and brown stains, food and wine. It is linen, with a pattern of vine leaves and clusters of grapes brocaded thickly all round the edges. It is always rather dirty, I have no facilities for boiling linen. It doesn't matter. I pull it up and dream.

When the light is yellower I wake up again and heat water in a saucepan for tea. I put the leaves in the boiling water. My saucepan has a lip, it is a good old saucepan, and it will last as long as I will. I will never lose it. I will lose nothing. I fetch a mug, a strainer and a tin of milk. If it is cold I get back into bed and drink two mugs of tea, warming my hands on the saucepan. I move my finger around the place where the enamel has cracked away. I know the shape very well. Sometimes, if it is bitter cold, I put my shawl round my shoulders, my scarf round my neck and ears, and carefully take the saucepan into bed so that it rests against my thighs, or on my stomach. Sometimes it has spilt. My bed smells of tea when my body warms it, spiced, it enters my sleep. There may be other smells less pleasing, but I cannot smell them, they are my odours.

The light gave me a dream this morning. In it I am a writer, striving, if such a word is right for the frivolity of writing, to express joy, fullness of joy: I have written many things in which I creep up on it and have told what it is sideways, inside-out, stories of misery, loneliness and sorrow, which show joy by its absence or loss. In the dream I have grown weary of this way and want to illuminate the paper on the table in front of me with the stuff itself. In the dream I think: how? And answer myself, describe, of course. I say to myself, well then: The sun shines in the window. Immediately the dream room has a window and light is shining in. It is lovely. It won't do for a dream-writer. The quality of the light must be described. I list attributes to write on my paper, and joy moves further away as I add to my list: bright, clear, golden, warm; fading, fading. I think: I eat toast and honey. Immediately there is toast and honey in front of me. I think: it is too simple, describe it; thick, hot, brown, crunchy; liquid, sweet, cheat-mellifluous; fading, fading. In my dream I get up from the table and the paper distressed because I'm failing and walk to the corner of the room near the window, I turn and look at the room and it is my room now and here it is, two chairs, clothes hanging on nails, bed with the wine-stained cover. It cannot be written.

I wake up remembering and make the saucepan of tea. I get up and wash my face in a little cold water. I enjoy washing my ears. I put on some clothes, I don't know what, there is not much choice, something warm because it is clear and lovely but cool, perhaps it is autumn or spring. Often I don't bother with knickers, sometimes my chest and back are bare. There is no one to see. I could go naked all day, on the porch too, if I wanted. People never pass. But today I wear clothes and grey socks on my feet.

I go first to open the door and see the splintered jamb. It is still there, I take my chair onto the wooden porch to sit. My eyes rest mostly on the wooden supports of the porch roof and the low sticks of wood with a handrail. Sometimes my eyes go further to the plain beyond my house. It takes a few moments before I see other than a blur, my eyes are growing old and unwilling to change focus. It makes them ache a little. The plain is fallow this year, perhaps it always is, I don't remember, some catch crop in part, some brown earth. It stretches as far as I can see, the same at the back of the house and the left and the right side. I can't see, but feel the emptiness. Maybe there was a time when I feared such spaces. The sky is very large. I can't see all of it because of the overhang of the porch roof. I watch clouds move slowly, the light change and thicken as the day wears at the wood, the road which no one walks, the fields of green and brown, so many browns, I rock a little in my chair, which I can do because I have set its back legs on a loose board, it gives, creaking, to my movement. I feel the rheumatism in my legs, no worse than usual, and pull my skirt up, apparently I put a skirt on; because the light is healing. I don't think. I learned a time ago, I don't remember how or when, that it is not necessary and can be stopped. I sit with the wood porch, the fields, the chair, the creak, the daylight, and they do not think any more than I do. There is a tree in the distance, good that it is a long way away. I can see it as a dark patch which obstructs the sky with the land, the land with the sky. But it is all right, it is very far away and I can fail to notice it.

My guts rumble to tell me they are empty. I am not hungry. The sky begins to fade. It is either late, or rain coming. It smells like rain. My legs chill and I cover them. I sit and watch the rain come dark and lovely from far away on the left. It moves across the plain and changes the greens and browns. It is an event. It moves my way. I shall have to go in when it reaches the house, the porch roof is full of holes, I like getting wet but have no way of drying myself. It comes and drops splatter through the roof. I carry my chair inside and sit by the window. I am not easy with the window frame. It cuts off the plain to a small picture. The plain is endless. If I turn to look into my room it is all right. My room is a small picture, mine, familiar, the cup joined by my thread to my bed, my old slippers joined to the door, everything known to everything by me.

The rain eases to a few drops and I go outside to the porch again with my chair. I never leave it out at night or when I move in again to make tea or a little food, it goes with me. I sit and watch a mauve and grey cloud at the end of the storm move slowly across the sky. It is so slow that I concentrate my eyes to see that it moves at all. It does so slowly. My eyes are not busy. Now I am able, in my age, to watch a drop of rain fall and land. Each one is shaped as a glass or crystal drop, round and heavy at the bottom and pulled to a thread at the top. Its landing on the porch is quiet and violent, it shatters. I believe that there was a time when I used to think: rain, storm, clouds; and that was that and that was all. I was busy.

I am hungry but not inclined to do anything about it yet. I shall know when the biscuits will taste best. I heat the tea left in the morning's saucepan and take my mug out to drink while I sit and rock while I choose between the splinter, the flakes, the raindrops; or the plain. It is a big choice to make. The dream recurs, which happens sometimes now. My eyes are not closed. Because I am awake, I suppose, it is changed. Though awake and asleep are not opposed as I believe there was a time when they used to be. Again here is the room, the table, the problem, the creation of the window with sunlight entering, the toast and honey. Again I turn to look in at the room. I stop dreaming on the instant because what I see is terrible. There is a figure in the room, in my room. She is there in answer to the dream problem of how to pen joy and I cannot allow her. I know her. I wake because she must disappear. I am badly upset and rock. The early morning dream of my room full of things handled and stained with me was perfect. This other dream is impossible. It is another place, another time, and that answer must be dead if the one I live by is to live. I am badly upset. My eyes ache from the sighting. She stood still, pale and slender, by the table, her hands at her side, what is worst looking at me as I looked at her. She was smiling, recognising me, but as always, I am forced to remember, not enough, not enough. The papers were gone from the table. There was only the plate with two slices of toast thick with honey, the plate was too small, the bread lapped over, honey was running slowly over the edge on to my table, and a spilling of crumbs. I am back there again. I remember it was she who ate sweet things, toast and honey, that was never one of my likings, it was hers.

I sit and rock and ache. The pain makes me forget my rheumatism. My face is stiff and pulled back, but I forget how to cry. I believe there was a time when I used to.

I shall never eat again. I haven't needed to for a long time, now I shall stop. I get up and fetch my chair in and go to bed. That's the best place. I mutter and sing a little to myself to cover the unbearable event. I don't know what: nonsenses that dispel, here we go gathering nuts in May on a cold and frosty morning. I lie there curled and humming and scratching at a small flake of skin to occupy myself. Nearly falling I suddenly get up and fetch my tins of milk, my tin of biscuits, my packets of rice and stumble with them to the door. I stand on the porch, I never go further, and throw them as far as I can across the plain. They are only comforts. I don't want them now. My bed remains. I don't want to suffer. But the time has come to discard comforts. I am surprised how well I can throw across the plain. Most of the foods leap from my hands and loop and arc like birds and carry themselves further than I think possible. The big tin of sweet biscuits is so heavy I can hardly lift it, last of all, to throw. It weighs down toward my porch. I manage to force it from my two hands. It falls only a few feet away, on the other side of the roadway where no one walks. It is the best I can do. I rest and see that the discards are nearly invisible on the browns and fallows of the wet ground. The biscuit tin is yellow and has not been lost. I have trained my eyes, which are still aching from a worse sight, to look across the plain. At the corner of my left eye I see a small movement: it could be a flying insect near but they do not usually come, or a bird further, but neither do they. With fear which I am in anyway I turn to look. A small figure is walking this way along the road. I crouch back and look as hard as I can. The focus comes and goes. I look at the wooden handrail six inches from me and force my eyes to clear the blur, they hurt like hell, and I pick hard at the flaked yellow paint. Some gets under my nails and sticks there and my finger ends bleed. It is no use. There is not time enough to tear my house apart before she reaches it. I go back in and close the door, it has no lock, I am lost, and get into bed. My bedcloth has fallen on the floor from the sudden getting up. It is caught on a nail in the wood. I pull desperately to get it up to cover myself with. It rips badly and stays however hard I pull fixed to the floor, but there is just enough when I curl small to cover myself, even my head. I shake. There is no path to my door, it is overgrown because I never go beyond the porch. Perhaps she will think it is a derelict house. I want absurdly to call out 'this house is empty'. I remember the shining yellow biscuit tin and her love of sweet things. My house might as well be made of gingerbread.

Her arrival on my porch is quiet and violent. Drops of water fall from my eyes. I am so used to silence I hear her blunt footsteps in soft shoes. I hear her put the tin down. She knocks.

She cannot come in. She must not go.

Sheba Feminist Publishers

Sheba is an independent feminist publishing co-operative which produces books by and for women. Our list includes titles under the following headings: fiction and poetry, sex and sexuality, books for younger readers, and on women in other countries, photographic books and feminist cartoons. All our titles are available from bookshops, or direct from Sheba Feminist Publishers, 488, Kingsland Rd, London E8. Please add 45p per volume for p & p. Send SAE to our address for a complete catalogue of books, postcards and posters.

Fiction/Poetry backlist

Smile Smile Smile Smile, Alison Fell, Stef Pixner, Tina Reid, Michele Roberts, Ann Oosthuizen.
Erotic, bitter, funny, bleak, thoughtful: a collection of poems, stories and drawings by a London-based feminist writers' group, who have gone on to individual success as novelists and poets.

'In the end it is the *content* of this collection which is exciting and radical – the making public, with pride, of all the previously censored experience of women. But the form is innovative too, and there are five very distinctive voices here – exuberant, full of energy, will and power.' *Tribune*

November 1980 £1.75 USA $4.95 128 pp 216 × 146 mm ISBN 0 907179 03 7

Feminist Fables, Suniti Namjoshi with illustrations by Susan Trangmar
'These short fables draw on well-known fairy tales and Greek and Sanskrit mythology, as well as original material, to remind us that the stories handed down to us aren't closed systems, but imaginative labyrinths for us to play in as we please.' *Gay News*

'Dear Sheba,
      I've just been given *Feminist Fables* by a friend – I'm only half-way through but I feel I have to write to let you know how brilliant I think it is. It makes me weep, it makes me laugh and smile and it also makes me feel that I'm reading something that I know all about, but have only just realised that I know it! A revelation in fact.' *Letter to Sheba*
Now translated into Chinese and Dutch. Reprinting.

April 1981 £3.25 USA $7.50 136 pp 186 × 123 mm ISBN 0 907179 04 5

Spitting the Pips Out, Gillian Allnutt
In this book Gillian Allnutt, now poetry editor of the radical London
weekly *City Limits*, writes in poetry and prose about her birth as a poet.

' . . . an unusual and effective mixture of prose, poetry and notes to herself,
all brilliantly woven together like a rich tapestry. Her book tells the story of
Eve, of her childhood with her brother and sister, her relationship with her
mother and her lover (Adam). Elegantly written, without ever being aloof,
it's a wonderfully rich, powerful book that may occasionally move you, as it
did me, to tears. Gillian evokes childhood games as well as adult ones with
that rare quality of allowing you to join her in a particular place and time.
And although it's Eve's (and Gillian's) story, parts of it seem to tell the
journey of us all.' *19 Magazine*

July 1981 £2.25 USA $5.25 128 pp 198 × 129 mm ISBN 0 907179 06 1

Loneliness and other Lovers, Ann Oosthuizen
Alternative best seller, now reprinted.
This compelling story of an older woman's discovery of feminism blows
away the doubts of women who might have heard women's liberation used
as a term of abuse. Far from losing her female-ness, Jean explores and
enriches her sexuality, her politics and her future options. Discarded by
her husband for a younger woman, she moves out of the suffocating
security of an oppressive marriage into a fuller, more challenging life.

'The women's movement stands in this novel in the position reserved for
the hero in another kind of romance: strong and perfect, but also
dangerous and exciting.' *Spare Rib*
'For a woman new to (or nervous of) the implications of feminism it should
provide a reassuring and encouraging introduction.' *City Limits*

Second Edition 1982 £2.75 USA $6.95 164 pp 198 × 129 mm

Everyday Matters, New Short Stories by Women
In 1982 Sheba advertised for women to send us short stories for a new
collection of women's writing. This book is our selection from those sent to
us. The stories describe and dissect our relationships with mothers, lovers,
husbands or friends – or with the state itself.

'If the conventional women's magazine stories offer a diet that's oversweet,
then this collection provides an antidote that includes a sharp dash of
bitters . . . daily life is closely inspected, turned inside out and well shaken
as part of the feminist process of telling the unconventional and often
uncomfortable truth.' *Michele Roberts, City Limits*

November 1982 £3.50 USA $7.95 160 pp 198 × 129 mm ISBN 0 907179 14 2

Between Friends, Gillian Hanscombe

'One of those rare books which manages to combine a powerful polemic with an intimate and engaging love story. The personal really is political for the four female protagonists, who attempt to mesh their often conflicting feminist theories with the facts of their own lives. And Gillian Hanscombe doesn't shirk these conflicts. Using a frank exchange of letters between the four, she explores a host of potentially explosive feminist positions – from that of Jane, an angry and passionate lesbian who believes that feminists should not raise boy children, to that of Amy who is fighting for the heterosexual revolution. In a world where there are no easy solutions, Gillian Hanscombe's achievement is to describe new ways in which women might live and fight together.' *Nicky Singer, Institute of Contemporary Art, London*

'A love story set in a battlefield mined with ideals . . . Risks and revolutions in friendships which are microcosms of the larger struggles of women . . .' *Off Our Backs*

March 1983 £3.95 180 pp 216 × 138 mm ISBN 0 907179 11 8